decker p.i.

BLOOD VOW

BILL CRAIG

Dedication:

To the brave men and women who are boots on the ground in the war against drugs, especially those in South Florida who are dealing with the scourge of Flakka...

Chapter One

It had been two weeks since Lacy Ryan's funeral. Sam Decker and Mark Mundy had both needed time to mourn the death of the woman that they loved. Sam as his fiancé and lover, Mark as a surrogate mother that he had only began to know. She had been murdered in front of them both by a contract killer for a drug lord called El Toro. She had been murdered at the funeral for Mark's father, DEA agent Kyle Mundy.

Sam and Mark had spent most of the time together until Sam decided that it was time for Mark to start back to school. He had sent him with Seminole Joe to a hidden island out in the middle of the Everglades where a lost tribe of Seminole Indians lived. They were called the hidden ones because they eschewed the ways of modern life, preferring the old ways. Monica Sinclair's little sister had moved to the island as well to work as a teacher to the youth of the Hidden Ones. She had welcomed Mark into the school and had assured both Sam and Joe that the boy would be safe and have a good education until it was safe for him to come out of the 'Glades and resume his life in a normal school.

Sam was sitting on the deck of his boat when Joe stepped aboard. He emptied the bottle of Killian's Red he had been drinking and dropped the glass bottle into a trash receptacle. He looked at Joe. "It's time," Decker said.

"Everybody is gathered at your house," Joe said. Decker closed his eyes. The house. It was supposed to have been for him and Lacy and Mark. Now, he wasn't sure he would be able to ever live in it. But it had been designated as the control center for what was about to happen. At least for the moment.

"Okay then, I guess we had better get over there then," Decker said.

"We should," Joe agreed. He made Decker get in his truck, rather than taking a chance on letting Decker drive himself. Joe was unsure if Decker might not try to kill himself since he blamed himself for Lacy's death.

Rafael Cortez frowned at the group gathered within Sam Decker's living room. He knew Wally Norwood, of course, and John Longfellow. The

5

older cowboy from Arizona was new, but he wanted to help. He had made it a point not to let his sister or Monica know about this meeting. He knew that neither of them would approve of what Sam planned to do, even though it was the right thing. Joe was supposed to bring Sam from his boat. Rafael hoped that they arrived soon. The sooner the better.

Rafael looked down at his watch. Joe and Sam were on the way. He looked at the other men. The room was quiet but filled with tension. He could understand that because he knew that it was a council of war. Because there was no way that Sam would let El Toro get away after murdering Lacy. He knew that Joe would call it a blood vow. The Italians would call it a vendetta. Rafael called it justice, and he was pretty sure that Sam would call it the same.

"They finally on the way, Wally?" Jake Baca asked. Jake Baca looked tired. His skin had the look of an old saddle after years spent under the desert sun. His once brown hair was now white. His clothes, from the snap fronted cowboy pattern shirt to his Levis were coated in dust as were the worn-down cowboy boots on his feet. The brown leather vest he wore had the same patina of dust and dryness. However, the gun tucked in the waistband of his trousers would be clean and oiled and dust free.

"I suspect they are, Jake. You didn't have to come, you know?" Wally Norwood replied.

"Sure, I did, Wally. Sam Decker did me a solid on that thing out in Arizona. He helped me out as well as helping his buddy," Baca replied.

"You used to be a smuggler," John Longfellow said accusingly.

"Don't throw stones, Johnny. You've crossed the line a few times yourself," Wally looked at the former Marshal.

"Yeah, I have. I'm not especially proud of that either," John sighed.

"Nobody in this room is without sin in some fashion or another. But we all owe Sam Decker in some fashion. So, let's not get bogged down with past crimes," Rafael said.

"Good point," Wally nodded. Wally was a Texas Ranger and Country Music icon that used his cover as a pot smoking musician to solve some pretty tough cases. Truth be told, he did enjoy the weed more than his bosses would approve of. A car pulled into the drive way. "They are here," Wally announced.

"Am I doing the right thing, Joe? By going in there?" Sam asked sitting in the passenger seat.

"They are all here because they want to help, Sam. They all want justice for Lacy as much as you do," Joe replied.

"I guess I knew that," Sam sighed.

"I guess you did too. However, you seem to want to do this by yourself. Sam, you need their help, otherwise it is just suicide. Mark needs you to survive it."

"I know that," Sam sighed.

"Do you?"

"I do. I want Justice for Lacy, but I want to live for Mark."

"That is what I needed to hear if I am to move forward on this with you," Joe said softly.

"Did you ever doubt it?" Decker asked.

"Not really, no," Joe replied. "But you were in more pain than I have ever seen you in. You are a strong man, but I was not sure that you were strong enough."

"To be honest, Joe, I didn't know if I was either. But El Toro has to pay for what he did. For Kyle, and for Lacy. I am going to bring his empire down around him and then I am going to piss on his smoking corpse," Sam Decker said quietly.

Joe felt a chill race down his spine as he looked into Decker's eyes. He was no longer seeing his friend, but instead a spirit of vengeance. For a very brief moment, he felt almost sorry for the drug lord known as El Toro. Almost. But not quite. Because he had loved Lacy Ryan in his own way too. Together they headed up the walk and then entered the house.

"Sammy," Wally Norwood said as he stepped inside.

"Wally. Hey, first thing, I want to tell you all thank you for coming. You don't have to be a part of this, but since you are here, I guess that means you want to be. I loved Lacy. She never should have had to die. Not that way. So I am going after El Toro. He has to pay for what he did," Decker said as he looked each man in the eyes.

"The best way to hurt this bastard is to hit him in the wallet," Jake Baca said. Decker nodded his agreement. "You know how he brings his drugs in?"

"I have a couple of ideas, but nothing solid. That is going to be the first order of business, finding his smuggling routes and shutting them down. Right now, he's the leading importer of Flakka in South Florida. I want his supply to dry up," Decker replied.

"I'll ask around. I've still got some contacts around from the old days,' Baca nodded.

"I appreciate it, Jake. We also need to pinpoint his warehouses and main base of operations."

"I can check on that through some of my contacts in the Marshal's Service," John Longfellow said.

"Good. We need to identify his street dealers too. I also want to find out who the man that pulled the trigger on Lacy was."

"I'll find the street dealers and where they work," Joe said.

"Rafael, I want you with me. We're going to drive up to Miami and rattle his cage. Plus, I want to talk to some of my old buddies in the DEA," Decker told his friend and business partner.

"I'm with you," Rafael nodded.

"Then I guess we all should get started," Decker said, ending the meeting. Everyone got up and headed for the door. Decker looked around the room.

"I don't know if I will ever be able to live here, Rafe. I was rebuilding it for a life with Lacy," Decker said.

"I know that, Sam. We haven't talked much since that day at the cemetery. I've been trying to respect that you needed some time and space to grieve," Rafael Cortez said softly.

"I'll finish grieving when El Toro is dead. You know where the fucking bastard lives?"

"I do."

"I need you to take me there, Rafe."

"Are you sure that is the best idea, Sam?"

"I need to see his face, Rafe. I need to look into his eyes and let him know what is coming. I'm going to war, with you or without you."

"I know that."

"I know you do, but I had to say it."

"I understand Sam. Every man that was in this room does. We all loved Lacy too. But I won't let you throw your life away by grandstanding."

"I'm not going to grandstand, and I'm not going to needlessly throw my life away. Mark needs me now more than ever, Rafe. I owe it to him to come out on the other side of this alive."

"As long as you remember that and don't get caught up in getting revenge at any cost."

"I won't, Rafe. I promise you that."

"Okay, so when do you want to head for Miami?" Rafael asked.

"Now seems like as good a time as any," Decker said.

"I'm worried, Nora," Monica Sinclair said, leaning back in her chair. Monica was the Chief of Police for Scorpion Cay.

"I am too. Sam has refused to see me or anybody else since Lacy was killed. He even had Joe take Mark out to the island of the Hidden Ones," Nora Santiago replied. Nora was Scorpion Cay's only police detective. She was also Monica's right hand.

"My sister is a teacher out there in the 'Glades," Monica said, just to be saying something.

"I know that. She offered to keep an eye on Mark and help him while he was grieving not only for his father but for Lacy as well. He had already accepted her as his mother to be," Nora said, shaking her head.

"I feel so sorry for that kid, he lost his dad and his prospective Mom in the course of a few days. He's gotta be fucked up by that."

"Your sister will help him with that."

"I know she will. But what the hell am I going to do about Sam?"

"You mean short of locking him in a cell until Lacy's killer is locked up?"

"Yeah," Monica sighed.

"You don't do anything. You let Sam do what he needs to do and you look the other way," Nora told her.

"Nora, if I catch Sam breaking the law, I can't look the other way. I will have to move on him. It's the law." Monica said softly.

"So, don't catch him, Monica. Lacy was your friend too. Do you really want to let her killer get away because it was done outside the rule of law?" Nora asked her.

"You know I don't, Nora."

"Then for the moment, you let Sam do his thing. If you see him crossing a line, then and only then do you act."

"If he crosses a line, it won't be here on the island."

"In that case, it won't be your problem, will it?"

"I guess not," Monica sighed. She could see the wisdom in what Nora was telling her, but she in no way thought it was right.

Red Jack frowned at El Toro. His boss was pleased that he had killed the woman, but Red Jack took no joy from it. She had not been his target. In fact, she was nothing more than collateral damage. He had missed both the boy and Sam Decker. Now, he had a bad feeling that it would come back to bite him on the ass.

"The woman is dead, El Jefe. I suspect that we may well have made a grave error," Red Jack said.

"I wanted to send a message, my friend. I wanted Sam Decker to know that I was not someone to be trifled with."

"I suspect that you might well have unleashed a demon on yourself." Red Jack told him.

"You think too much of this private eye," El Toro scoffed. "He is too busy licking his wounds to be concerned with me."

"I can only hope you are right, El Jefe."

"I am always right, Red Jack," El Toro laughed.

CHAPTER TWO

Jake Baca headed for Miami. He knew it was a three-hour drive but that wasn't that big a deal. There were people he needed to talk to. They would be able to tell him how El Toro was bringing his drugs into Miami. They might not be too eager to help at the beginning, but they would by the time that he was done. Jake liked and respected Decker, had since the first time that he had encountered him. Plus, he owed both him and Wally for getting all the charges against him in Texas dropped. That had allowed him to go home. That was a debt he could never pay.

Jake had been a smuggler in Arizona and Texas for years. Usually he just moved pot across the border, sometimes cash. But he never moved cocaine or anything heavy, and he drew the line at moving people. He had seen too many of the victims of coyotes left for dead among the trails heading north into the United States. But people like El Toro? They had no consciences. They didn't care as long as they made money, just like the cartels. That was why he had gotten out of the game.

Smuggling had gone from being a thrill to being a very deadly and dangerous business. Jake had gotten out while he still had a chance to. He had helped Decker find an old friend that had been kidnapped by the Cartels out in Arizona, a former DEA agent. In fact; the man that had introduced them. As a result, Decker and Wally had got all outstanding warrants against him in Texas quashed. So, he owed them. When he had seen the television reports of Lacy Ryan's death, he had got on the first flight to Florida and headed for Scorpion Cay. Because Jake knew what kind of man Sam Decker was. He knew that Decker would need help to get the man responsible for Lacy's death.

The first guy he wanted to talk to was Emilio Hernandez. Emilio had a hand in all the drugs that came through Miami and he would know about El Toro.

John Longfellow sat in his motel room looking at the telephone. He had mixed emotions about this business. But he owed Sam Decker. Sure, he had helped Decker in the past, when Decker had been framed for the murder of his ex-wife, but this time it was different.

This time he was actively involved in the planning of another man's murder. Because he had no doubt that once Decker had the opportunity; that he planned to execute El Toro. But Lacy Ryan had not deserved to die. Especially not by an assassin's bullet. John picked up the phone and started punching buttons, dialing a number that part of him didn't want to call…

Wally Norwood was on his private plane, flying from Key West to Miami. He hadn't told Sam what he was going to do, but he figured that was for the best. Sam hadn't really designated a job for him and Wally knew why. Sam knew that Wally would coordinate behind the scenes to make sure that no government agencies interfered with Sam's plans for El Toro.

Personally, he wanted to rip the man's head off and shit down his neck. Wally would have no problem with staking El Toro out on an ant hill and pouring honey all over him. He had liked Lacy, had known that she was what Sam had needed. Now she was gone, and Sammy was adrift on a stormy sea. Wally also worried for young Mark, caught in a war that he didn't understand. That boy had suffered far more than anyone else. Wally wanted to make sure that he had at least a fighting chance for a future. Sam Decker could give him that, if Sam survived.

Seminole Joe also drove north. El Toro had people on the streets to move his product. He would find them and identify them. And when the time came, he would remove them. It was time to send a message to El Toro that he was not invincible.

Joe also knew that El Toro would die. Sam Decker was consumed by a spirit of Vengeance. That spirit would not stop until El Toro was dead.

Sam Decker might die as well, but it would not be until El Toro was cold and dead on the street...

"Sam, are you sure this is the right thing to do?" Rafael asked.

"Are you getting cold feet?" Decker asked his voice low and soft.

"No. But I want to know where your head is at."

"You have that right."

"I know I do. So, Sam, where is your head at?"

"Lacy should not have died."

"I know that, Sam. But she did."

"Yes, she did. El Toro ordered her death, Rafe. I can't let him get away with that."

"I know that too."

"Lacy didn't need to die. But El Toro has to pay for what he or his men did."

"I get that."

"Do you, Rafe? I'm not so sure."

"Dammit Sam, I loved her too. Not like you did, but I loved her too."

"I know you did. She had that effect on people. Lacy was one of a kind."

"She was," Rafael agreed.

"Wake me when we get close to El Toro's place," Decker told him.

"I will," Rafael told him.

Red Jack was disturbed. From what he had seen of Sam Decker he had a bad feeling that hell itself would soon descend on Miami. While he worked for El Toro, he would do his best to protect him. But he would not throw away his own life for El Toro if it came down to it. Red Jack knew that discretion was the better part of valor and he had no problem with packing up his tent and disappearing into the night if things got too hot in Miami.

His boss wouldn't understand, would probably even brand him a traitor and a coward for it. But Red Jack didn't care. It was better to be a live coward than a dead hero, especially if it meant dying for a foolish mistake. He had no doubt that Sam Decker would be coming for them. Decker's reputation made it a sure thing. He would come to avenge his woman. If El Toro thought otherwise, El Toro was a damned fool!

Sam Decker's mind was adrift. Memories flitting in and out of his consciousness. The first time he had ever seen Lacy. Their first kiss. The first time that they had made love. Times on his boat. The day he had proposed to her and she had said yes. And finally, that day in the cemetery at Kyle Mundy's funeral. The attack by El Toro's men. The moment that the bullet had punched through Lacy as she attempted to shield Mark with her own body. Her there on the ground, blood covering her torso, leaking out of her mouth.

Seeing her breathe her final breath as the light had faded from her eyes.

Decker jerked away, his heart pounding, sweat beading on his forehead. "You okay?" Rafael asked from the driver's seat.

"Yeah, just a bad dream," Decker replied. He wished he had a cigarette and he wished he had a drink. The cigarette to calm his nerves, and the whiskey to help deaden the pain in his heart. But now wasn't the time. He had to keep a clear head, especially now that he was getting ready to take the fight to El Toro.

"Sam, you're my brother. You sure you are up for this right now?" Rafe asked, shooting him a glance.

"I am, Rafe. I need to see this son of a bitch face to face. I need to look him right in the eye."

"You know that he might just shoot us and not bother talking?"

"It's a chance I'm willing to take. El Toro's ego will get in the way. He'll see us so he can lord his power over us. I just want to send him a message and tell him how little I care about his so-called power," Decker said.

"Okay. I just want to make sure that you know that there is a possibility of things going south. You seem to know that," Rafael replied.

"I'm very aware of it, Pal," Decker sighed.

"Johnny, you know I could get into a world of trouble for giving you this info. You're fucking retired," Anson Moore told him.

"I know that, Anson. I wouldn't be asking if it wasn't really important," Longfellow told his old friend.

"Yeah, I get that. This have anything to do with that lawyer getting shot down there on Scorpion Cay?"

"It does. Her fiancé is a friend of mine and I owe him."

"I figured it was something like that. You aren't much of one to ask for favors, unlike a lot of the other guys retired from the service."

"This is the first time I have ever asked," John Longfellow said.

"I know that too, Johnny. That's why I'm going to give you what you want. I just hope that it won't come back to bite me on the ass."

"It won't."

"I gonna hold you too that, Johnny."

"I know that," Longfellow told him.

Joe had parked his car in a parking garage and had hit the streets. He was a ghost as he moved along the streets of Miami. He saw a lot and interfered with nothing. Most folks ignored him, other than a few who were intimidated by his size alone.

He could move about quicker on foot. He could also check out more dealers that way. El

Toro was a big man in Little Havana and that was where Joe had decided to focus his attention.

"We are here, Sam," Rafael said from the driver's seat. Sam Decker opened his eyes. He had been dreaming about Lacy. Decker rubbed his eyes and sat up, twisting his neck, popping it.

"So, let's go inside the gate," Decker said.

"In case you haven't noticed, the gate is steel and it is closed."

"Like I'm really going to let that stop me. Turn the car around and join me on the other side of the gate."

"Sam, I'm not so sure this is a good idea."

"I need to look this fucker in the eyes, Rafe. I need to let him know what is coming."

"I get that Sam, I really do. But why his house late at night?"

"Because he needs to know that there is no place that I won't be able to go after him," Decker climbed out of the car and moved to the gate. Rafael shook his head and turned the car around. By the time, he had gotten out of his car, Decker was already over the gate.

Sam Decker waited while Rafael clambered over the steel gate. "I hope we don't have to climb it if we have to leave in a hurry," Rafael groused.

"Exercise is good for you," Decker grinned at him. It was good to see him smile. It hadn't happened a lot in the past few weeks.

Maybe Sam wasn't totally being consumed by revenge. It gave Rafael something to hold onto. Anything was good.

Mateo Salvador drained the glass of Cuban Rum. He was riding high the past two weeks. While Red Jack had moaned, and complained about killing the woman, El Toro knew that it had been the right thing to do. It had sent a message to Sam Decker, had told him that El Toro was no one to trifle with, that he, El Toro, was the Kingpin of South Florida!

He picked up his cigar and puffed on it as he walked back to the bar to refill his drink. Rum from his homeland was now readily available in Miami thanks to President Obama. He toasted the American president before taking another sip of the sweet Cuban beverage. He loved the feel of the burn as it worked down his throat and exploded into his belly before spreading out to the rest of his body.

He had already increased his imports of the Chinese made Flakka that were coming up through the keys. It was making him a large fortune in far less time than cocaine had during the old days. He heard a noise from the French doors and turned to see what it was. Two men stood there. One Gringo, one who looked Cuban.

"Hey there, El Toro," Sam Decker smiled. He pulled out his Browning Hi-Power 9mm and thumbed back the hammer. "Do you know who I am?"

"I think you are a dead man." Mateo Salvador said softly.

"You'd be wrong, Matty baby. I'll still be here long after the worms have consumed your rotting flesh," the Gringo said.

"Do you know who I am?" Salvador asked, puffing up. He was not used to being disrespected like this.

"I know exactly who you are. You're a scum sucking drug dealer that murdered my fiancé. I'm Sam Decker you motherfucker. I want you to know, I am going to be coming after you and I will destroy your operation, and I will destroy you. Killing Lacy was the biggest mistake you have ever made," Decker told him.

"So, you are Decker. Who the fuck cares? You are nothing to me," Salvador spat.

"Oh, but I will be. Because I'm going to cut the horns off the bull," Decker said, crossing the room in two fast steps and lashing out with his gun. El Toro hit the ground, blood dripping from his face. The two men were gone, vanished like ghosts in the night.

Chapter Three

"My God, I wouldn't have believed it if I hadn't seen it with my own fucking eyes!" Rafael shook his head as he drove them out of the area.

"It really wasn't that big a deal, Rafe," Decker told him.

"Bullshit, Sam."

"Why is that?"

"I saw real fear in his eyes, Sam. I've never seen that on the face of El Toro or any of his men before," Rafael replied.

"Good. I want him to be afraid. Because if he's afraid, he might make a mistake," Decker explained.

"You are too close to this, Sam. You know it, I know it, and so does everyone else. Everybody loved Lacy, Sam."

"Don't try to talk me out of this Rafe. I will avenge both Lacy and Mark's dad," Decker replied.

"I couldn't talk you out of it if I tried, Sam. We both know that. But I can try to stop you from taking some pretty damn foolish chances," Rafael replied.

"I'm sure you could," Decker replied.

"Sam," Rafael looked at him.

"Old El Toro is going to die, Rafe. He murdered Lacy and he murdered Kyle. He is going to pay for that."

"I get that, Sam. I really do. But you have got to be more careful in your approach to this."

"Why?"

"Because El Toro has a reputation for being one of the most vicious drug lords in South Florida."

"He's going to find out what real viciousness is, Rafe. I will terrorize this son of a bitch before I make him pay!"

"I know you will. All I am asking is that you don't throw your own life away while doing so. If anything happens to you, where will that leave Mark?"

Decker thought about that for a long moment. "You're right Rafe. I have to put Mark ahead of my own wishes and desires."

"I know that, Sam. I just wanted to make sure that you did as well," Rafael said.

"I want to kill that son of a bitch, but at the same time, I need to protect Mark from whatever fallout that comes along," Decker said.

"I know that too, Sam."

"I know you do, Rafe."

"So, what the fuck is next, Sam?"

"We start knocking out all of his operations, Rafe," Decker replied.

"Okay," Rafe nodded.

John Longfellow entered the club. He was still uncomfortable, but he owed Wally and he owed Decker. He made his way to the bar and ordered a Scotch neat. The bartender returned with it in a couple of minutes. John tossed it back and waited. When the bartender came back he ordered another. He would take his time with this one, because he needed to gather information, and he couldn't do that if he got shit-faced drunk.

He kept one eye on the door and when Manny Solares entered the bar, he picked up his drink and walked to the table that Solares was headed for. Solares recognized him. So, he wasn't surprised when John dropped into the seat across from him.

"To what do I owe this pleasure, Deputy Marshal?" Solares asked.

"I'm looking for information, Manny," Longfellow told him.

"About what?"

"About a Mexican drug dealer who calls himself El Toro and is importing a lot of Flakka into the States.

"You are asking a lot, Marshal Longfellow."

"El Toro killed a good friend of mine. I could give a shit if he lives or dies, but he needs to pay for what he did," Longfellow said.

"I get that. I heard about it. Sam Decker's woman, wasn't she?"

"She was. But she was also a friend of mine too," Longfellow told him

"El Toro is pretty full of himself. He seemed to think that if he took out Decker's woman that Decker would back off," Manny Solares sighed.

"He was wrong. Sam Decker never backs down," Longfellow said.

"I get that now. El Toro thinks that he is sitting pretty and that nobody will stand up to him."

"I suggest that you take a vacation, Manny. Things are about to get very hot in South Florida," Longfellow told him.

"I figured as much. I'm sorry I can't help you more."

"I know that. Goodbye, Manny. I hear California is quieter this time of year."

"That sounds like a very good idea," Manny said before he took off.

John Longfellow sighed. He knew that there was no way in hell that Sam Decker would back off. El Toro was a dead man walking, he just didn't know it. Lots of people wanted the dealer dead, for many reasons. But several of them were personal. And those were the ones that would pursue El Toro until he died.

Wally Norwood sat in a Miami bar. The name was unimportant. However, what was important was the fact that Sam Decker was looking for a drug dealer named El Toro. El Toro was directly responsible for the death of Sam Decker's finance. Wally swore that he would find El Toro for Sam. Dead or alive. He'd prefer to find the guy dead before Sam could get to him. Because he knew that if Sam found him first, Sam would cross a line that he should never have to cross.

That was not something that Wally ever wanted Sam to face. Because of Wally, Decker's father had been forced to cross that line. In the end, it had cost him his life. Sam deserved better than that. Wally picked up his tumbler of Jim Beam and took a drink. He liked the way that the melted ice diluted it without diluting the flavor, or the burn as it went down.

Sometimes a man needed a drink of good bourbon to get him through hard times. For Sam, the times couldn't get much harder. Wally had never seen a couple more in love than Sam and Lacy. They had deserved a chance at happiness if anyone did. But that had been torn away from them. Lacy was dead. Sam had become a murderous weapon of vengeance. Wally only hoped that he could save the man that he had come to think of as a son.

"So, what is next?" Monica Sinclair asked.
"What do you mean?" Nora Santiago asked.
"For Sam and that brother of yours! I know that Rafael is in this with Sam up to his eyeballs!" Monica said.

"I have no idea what you are talking about," Nora replied.

"Nora."

"I don't know anything, Monica."

"You had better be telling me the truth, Nora."

"I am. If you have any doubts, you can have my badge right now," Nora said. Monica believed her.

"Okay, Nora. I believe you," Monica said softly.

"I hope so, Monica. Because if you don't, then maybe I don't know you as well as I thought I did."

"On the plus side, we no longer have Flakka moving on our streets, or being transported through here."

"A little bit of goodness at least. Lacy didn't die for nothing at least."

"I wonder if she would say the same thing. Can you have your brother tell Sam to call me at least?" Monica asked.

"I can text him," Nora nodded.

"You do that, Nora. I really need to talk to Sam."

"I know that. I'll do what I can, Monica."

"I know you will, Nora."

Sam Decker checked into the Miami hotel room. So far, nobody knew who he was. But Sam also knew that was about to change. Decker knew that once he started this personal war with El Toro that a lot of folks would know who he was. They would also know why he did what he did and why he managed to disappear every time the cops got close.

What he was doing was crossing the line, moving from being a good guy into being a bad guy. He was going to kill El Toro. That was a given. It was revenge for Lacy's death. Kyle too. He hoped that it would bring peace for both himself and Mark.

"You sure that was the smart play, Sam?" Rafael asked.

"It was for me. I want him too angry to see straight," Decker replied.

"I figured that," Cortez told him.

"If he's angry, he won't be smart. I need him not to be smart," Decker shrugged.

Salvador was furious as he called for his men. The ones who were supposed to be protecting him from assholes like this Sam Decker and his silent friend! He had expected some push back after the death of the woman, but Decker coming to his house, that was not expected. He had thought that killing the woman, the person Decker cared most about, would scare the private investigator away from his business for good. It appeared he had underestimated Decker. He would not do that again!

The thing about drug dealers is they like to think they are untouchable because the cops haven't been able to make a case against them. That usually only applies to the ones at the top. The street level dealers know they are at risk, even in their own territory. Any customer could potentially be an undercover cop or somebody looking to rip them off. They are especially wary of new faces looking to do business.

So, the best way to approach one of them is right after they have made a sale and from a spot where they cannot see you coming. Which is the approach that Joe chose to use. For a six-foot four-inch tall Seminole Indian, Joe could move and disappear like a Ninja.

The dealer was totally unprepared when a large hand encircled his neck and pulled him into the ally. He was even less prepared for the cold touch of a knife blade on his throat.

"What do you want," the dealer bleated like a goat. Joe smiled and it was pure menace.

"Do you work for the man called El Toro?" Joe asked, his voice a low rumble that was as sibilant as a snake's hiss.

"Ye-yes."

"You are going to take me to where you have your Flakka stashed."

"El Toro will kill me if I do that," the dealer shook his head.

"You'll be dead if you don't," Joe told him, putting just enough pressure on the knife blade to break the skin and start a trickle of blood flowing, but not enough pressure to do any real damage. The kid gave him the information that he needed. Joe vanished into the night. He had other calls to pay!

Monica Sinclair frowned as she looked at the paperwork on her desk. This was doing nothing to discover who had murdered Lacy Ryan. She was worried about Decker. She had never seen him like he had looked at Lacy's funeral. He was colder than an iceberg. So was the boy, Mark. That kid had seen too much in his short life. She knew Sam was hurting. He had loved Lacy beyond life. But she knew that the kid was hurting too. He had lost not only his father, but his new mother as well.

Monica picked up her coffee and sipped from the mug. Sam had left the island, and she was fairly certain that he had gone to Miami. Because that was where El Toro was. She sighed. Sam was on his own once he left the island, and there was not a goddam thing that she could do to help him!

Chapter Four

Jake Baca walked up behind Benito Guevara and grabbed him by the neck, slamming his face into the bar. The bartender paid no attention, giving them nothing more than a bored glance. Blood was dripping from Bennie's nose as Baca released him. "Benny, long time no see," Baca told him.

"What the hell, Jake?" Guevara demanded, rubbing the blood draining out of his nose.

"You know a local honcho called El Toro?" Baca asked.

"I know who he is."

"You sell any of his product?"

"Why you want to know, Jake?"

"Because I asked. I still remember how you fucking set me up in Juarez, Bennie."

"I never thought of you as being the kind that carried a grudge, Jake."

"I have a beef with El Toro. I want to know where he gets his product."

"If I tell you that and he finds out, El Toro will kill me," Benito said.

"If you don't tell me I'll cut you from crotch to brisket right here and now. It's your choice," Baca told him softly. He edged his coat back to where Benito could see the bone-handled Bowie knife secured on his belt. Benito's eyes went wide with fear.

"Okay, I'll tell you, but you didn't get this from me."

"You tell me the truth, you get a pass. You lie to me or set me up, you'll never see me coming," Baca hissed softly. Benito pissed his pants as he told Baca what he wanted to know. "Go home and clean up, Bennie. You're fucking disgusting," Baca shook his head. He left the bar.

Even this long after dark, the night was hot and humid. There had been storms earlier in the evening. Miami reminded him why he hated big cities. He had a lead on where El Toro kept his stash, but he wanted to verify the information from other sources first, before he called Sam and let him know.

"I told you killing the woman was a mistake," Red Jack told Mateo Salvador.

"You are not hearing me. Sam Decker came here, into my home! I want you to find him and kill him! I want it to be your top priority!" Mateo shouted.

"And it shall be, El Jefe. But it will take time. Miami is a big place," Red Jack told him.

"I know that," Mateo Salvador sighed.

"I just want you to know, this will not be an easy thing to accomplish."

"I know that. I want him dead, Amigo!"

"I know that as well, Jefe." Red Jack sighed as he headed out of the room. He would hit the streets and see what he could find out.

Seminole Joe had managed to spot at least half a dozen of El Toro's dealers and he knew where they picked up their supply of the product and where they went to sell it. He was quietly building a profile of how El Toro's men operated for Sam Decker. It reminded Joe of recon missions he had run way back as a young man during Vietnam.

His lips twitched in a brief smile. Wally and Jake Baca were older than him but not by much, yet Joe knew he looked younger and in better shape than either of them. Part of that came from the natural foods he ate while living out in the glades, part of it was genetic heritage.

He worried about his friend Sam Decker. The violent death of a loved one could affect a man in many ways, depending on how strong they were in spirit. Sam had a strong spirit, but he was also grieving and open to angry spirits that might chose to invade him and make him do violent acts that he might ordinarily no consider. Sam would make him a medicine pouch, something that he would the angry and evil spirits at bay until Decker had completed his quest to bring the men responsible for Lacy's death to justice.

The Everglades, Island of the Hidden Ones.

Mark Mundy sat by himself in a corner of the dining hall. He had his back in the corner and his knees bent up in front of his face, his blond hair hanging down over his face, which was hidden behind crossed arms. He felt so alone. Sure, there were lots of kids here, but they were very different from him. They all had families. He had lost his mother a few years back. Now his father was dead. So was Miss Lacy. He felt the tears starting to leak from his eyes and he brushed his arm across his face, angrily trying to wipe away tears before anybody noticed them and started calling him a cry baby.

He was alone now, and he had to make himself hard against a hard world. He had to be strong, even though he wanted nothing more than to be held and cuddled and told that everything would be okay. Except it would never be okay again. He was an—an orphan now! He hated the sound of the word. Hated it and everything that it implied. He squeezed deeper into the corner, sobbing silently at what his life had become.

Julia Sinclair watched Mark Mundy from across the dining hall. She was worried for him. No child should ever have to face what he was facing. She had promised both Sam and Joe that she would take care of him, try to help him process what had happened to him. She had known at the time that it wouldn't be easy. It was, she decided, time to start doing what she could for the young boy. Julia stood and walked across the room and knelt down in front of Mark. "Do you want to talk about it?" she asked, keeping her voice light.

"Talk about what?" Mark snuffled, wiping his nose on his wrist and glaring at her defiantly.

"About whatever it is that led you to come over here and sit by yourself," Julia replied

"It's private," Mark said, his voice heating up.

"So, you are saying that you don't want to share it with me?"

"That's right."

"Sometimes talking about things helps."

"You say. Why should I talk about it?"

"Because, sometimes getting things off your chest allows you to see it a little differently," Julia explained.

"Why did Mr. Sam send me here? He said he was going to take care of me."

"Because he wants you to be safe while he finds the people who killed your Dad and Miss Lacy," Julia said softly. Her throat felt thick as she spoke.

"He just wants me out of the way, just like Daddy did when he went after the bad men!" Mark snapped his face red with anger.

"Mark, that's not true at all! Your father loved you! He didn't want you getting hurt. Sam doesn't want you to get hurt either," Julia told him.

"So, he sent me away! What happens if Mr. Sam doesn't come back either?" Mark demanded. Julia opened her mouth and then closed it. Because she didn't have an answer for that. Instead she slipped her arms around Mark and pulled him against her, holding him tight.

Miami, Florida.

Dan Costa looked up as his door opened and Sam Decker walked in. He noticed that at least Decker had gotten a visitor's badge before charging into his office. "Sam Decker, to what do I owe the displeasure?"

"Dan, is that anyway to greet and old pal?" Decker asked, dropping into the seat across the desk from the DEA agent.

"Sam, we were never pals. In fact, I could never stand you. Kyle liked you though, so that buys you something," Costa said.

"You know I am Mark's guardian?"

"Yeah, well Kyle never made really good decisions."

"Dan," Decker glared across the desk.

"What do you want, Sam?"

"I want everything you can give me on Mateo Salvador," Decker said.

"You don't want much, do you?" Costa shook his head.

"Dan, I'm doing this as much for Mark as I am for me. That boy needs to know that the man that murdered his father was brought to justice."

"Do you plan to bring him to justice, Sam? Or do you plan to shoot him on sight?" Costa asked.

"If I wanted to do that, he would already be dead, Dan. I've already been to see Salvador, and I put him on notice."

"You didn't? Oh my God, you did! Do you even know how fucking lucky you are to be alive, Sam?"

"I'm not that easy to kill, Dan. I am going to bring Mateo Salvador in, dead or alive. And I will do it by the book," Decker said.

"Sure you will, Sam. I believe in the tooth fairy too."

"It's always good to believe in something," Decker said as he stood and walked out of the office.

"Son of a bitch," Dan Costa said, shaking his head. He hadn't expected that from Sam Decker. Costa was well aware of Decker's reputation. He was also pretty sure that there wasn't a cop in South Florida who wasn't. Costa turned in his chair and started tapping on his computer's keyboard. Within minutes he sent everything on Mateo Salvador, a.k.a. El Toro, to Sam Decker's e-mail address. Things were about to heat up in Miami. One way or another!

Rafael Cooper listened to his sister on his cell phone as he waited for Decker to emerge from the local DEA headquarters in Miami. "I'll do what I can," Rafael told him.

"Please do, because Monica really wants to talk to him," Nora said.

"I don't doubt that at all."

"What?" Decker asked as he slid into the passenger seat of Cortez's car.

"Monica wants you to call her. That was Nora passing along the message," Rafael said.

"I really don't have anything to talk to her about right now," Decker said stiffly.

"I know you still blame Monica for letting El Toro and his men get away after Lacy was killed, but you need to let that go. She and the police force did everything they could against a force with superior fire-power."

"I don't blame her for that. I blame myself."

"Sam."

"Let's change the subject okay? Any word from the others?" Decker asked.

"Not yet. Is your DEA buddy going to help?"

"He is. When we get back to the hotel room, it should be on my laptop," Decker replied.

"That will help," Rafael nodded as he put the car in gear and then pulled out into the traffic. Decker's cell phone rang.

"Go," Decker answered.

"I've got a location on a couple of his stash houses," Jake Baca reported.

"Good. Head for the hotel. I sent the address earlier."

"I got it. Now what?"

"Once every body reports in we start planning this war on El Toro and his operation," Decker replied.

Chapter Five

Joe was leaning against the wall of the hotel when Rafael pulled up, looking as if he owned the place. He nodded as Sam and Rafael climbed out of the car. "I have news," Joe said, his voice a deep rumble as if he was speaking from the bottom of a deep well, though pitched low enough that only they could hear them.

"It can wait until everybody gets here," Decker clapped him on the shoulder as the three of them headed for the interior doors. They were an odd trio, the red-haired American, the dark-skinned Cuban, and the Native Seminole American. People regarded them with curiosity as they made their way to the elevator and then vanished inside it.

Wally Norwood shook hands with the Miami-Dade Police Director Juan Perez. "Thank you, Juan for your cooperation in this matter," Wally said.

"I can't say I'm thrilled about it, Wally. But I've worked with you before and I know Sam Decker's reputation both from his days in the DEA and as a private investigator. If there is anything that my people can do to help, rest assured that we will. Flakka is a scourge that we need to eliminate. I'll check with my narcotics unit and see if they have anything that might be of help," Perez told him.

"I appreciate that, Juan. You know how to reach me," Wally told him.

"I do. I expect tickets to your next show when you're in town."

"You've got 'em," Wally grinned as he turned and walked out of the office. His phone vibrated as he headed for the entrance. Wally pulled it out and answered it.

"I have what the Marshal's had on Salvador, Wally. I can't say I am happy about it though," John Longfellow's voice filled his ear.

"Johnny, none of us are happy about it. We owe it to both Sam and Lacy to see it through," Wally replied.

"I guess."

"Head for the hotel room that Sam rented. Make sure you aren't followed," Wally told him before breaking the connection. He didn't want to give the former Deputy U.S. Marshal a chance to complain about what they were doing. He had heard enough of it already. Once he was outside he climbed in to his rental car and headed out into traffic.

It was near midnight when Jake Baca arrived at the hotel. Wally pulled in right behind him. Wally looked over the parking lot. Johnny hadn't arrived yet. He frowned. While Johnny had cleared Sam's name when he was set up for his ex-wife's murder, Decker had also saved John's life on a couple of occasions. If Johnny backed out, Wally knew that he would find him and chew him a new asshole!

"You been keeping out of trouble you old reprobate?" Jake asked.

"There ain't no fun in that," Wally laughed.

"Ain't that the truth," Jake agreed, laughing as well.

"It is." Together they entered the hotel and made their way to the elevator.

"Are we going to have problems from the cops?" Jake asked.

"Not unless things go really sideways. You find anything?" Wally asked.

"I found a lot. It should be real interesting when we all pool our information."

"I'm sure it will be. Once it is all laid out, you can bet that Sammy will come up with a plan of attack that will have old El Toro rocking on his heels."

"If it doesn't, I'm pretty damn sure we can add our own frills and whistles that will turn El Toro's suppliers against him," Jake said.

John Longfellow sat in the bar looking at the glass of whiskey sitting in front of him. He realized that he was supposed to be driving to the meeting where Decker had taken rooms for them all, but he just couldn't bring himself to do it. Not yet. Wally was going to be disappointed in him, Sam as well, if he didn't show. Except he had to ask the question, could he live with himself if Decker did shoot El Toro down where he found him?

It stuck in his craw and he hated it. Murder was not something he could overlook. If he saw Sam Decker shoot El Toro down in cold blood, he would have to arrest him. Part of himself hated him for feeling that way. El Toro had ordered his men to shoot down Kyle Mundy in front of his son. El Toro had been responsible for the attack at Kyle Mundy's funeral that had resulted in Lacy Ryan's death.

John picked up the glass and tossed it back, motioning the bartender for another. Maybe if he got too drunk to make the drive, he would avoid having to make a choice.

Everglades, Island of the Hidden Ones.

Julia Sinclair sat beside Mark Mundy's bed. He had finally eaten and gone to sleep. Still, she worried about him. She had heard from the woman that watched over the sleeping quarters that he had awakened from nightmares screaming and that it was upsetting the other children, even though that they had been told he had watched both his parents die.

So tonight, she was in a chair beside his bed, ready to comfort him if the nightmares came back. If he woke up screaming in the middle of the night.

Mark Mundy had seen far more than any child should have to witness. He had watched his mother die from a rare form of brain cancer. He had saw his father murdered, shot down in front of him. He had seen the woman that had cared for him afterward, shot down in cold blood. That was too much for any child to deal with.

So here she was. Julia had made a promise, not only to Sam Decker, the man that had saved her life[1], but to Seminole Joe as well. Joe had been the one who had first brought her to the island of the Hidden Ones. Joe had shown her that she needed to put others before herself and had taught her to become a teacher for the children.

It had brought here a sense of peace and serenity that she had never before experienced. Out here on the island, Julia knew that she mattered. She couldn't say the same for out in the world. Her students loved her. They adored her because of her compassion and love for them.

If Mark still had problems, she would have call Sam and let him know about it. Mark needed a counselor that was good with kids and helping them through grief and just growing up.

Mark also held a lot of anger inside. Julia had to find a way to help him deal with that anger. Because if he didn't get help with it, that anger could consume him!

---

[1] Decker P.I. Smuggler's Blues

Miami, Florida.

Enchufe rojo or Red Jack, in English, paced the floor. He was worried. El Toro was livid at the invasion of his home by Sam Decker. On the plus side, at least Mateo was taking his security suggestions to heart. He had called in men and had beefed up security around his residence and at the office where he conducted his legitimate 'cover' business.

Red Jack had known going after Decker's woman and the boy had been a mistake. He was all too aware of Sam Decker's reputation as both a private investigator and his days working for the Drug Enforcement Administration. He was going to be a formidable foe.

Bad news was already roiling in as tales of a giant Indian attacking some of the street level Flakka dealers and destroying their stashes of the drug. The cops were cracking down as well.

Enchufe Rojo had put more men on the street, searching for Sam Decker, but so far, they had not had any luck in locating him. The one thing that was certain was that Decker had left Scorpion Cay. Nobody seemed to know where he was or what had happened to the boy. It was very puzzling.

John Longfellow took a deep breath as he walked down the hallway looking for the door to the room that Decker had rented under an assumed name. He was here because he owed Decker. Owed him his life. He was going to make it clear that there were lines that he wouldn't cross. He hoped that Sam would understand. He found the room and pulled the key card out of his pocket. He used it to unlock the door and stepped inside.

Decker and the rest were inside waiting. John could feel the butterflies in his stomach as he walked up to Decker and handed him the manila file folder. "This is what the Marshal's had on Mateo Salvador, Sam. I can't say I am comfortable with being a part of all this," he said.

"I understand that John. I wouldn't ask you to do anything you couldn't live with. If I wanted El Toro dead, I would have done that when Rafael and I dropped in on him last night. I want to bring him to justice, not go after revenge. That's what Lacy would want me to do," Decker replied.

"I'm glad to hear that, Sam. Because if you were to kill him in cold blood I'd have no choice to arrest you."

"I know that John, and I respect it. But killing El Toro won't bring Lacy or Kyle back. So, instead, I am going for justice for both of them. As Rafael, and now you, have reminded me, it is the right thing to do."

"Then let's start figuring out our plan of attack," Longfellow said, breathing a silent sigh of relief. He would hate to take any of the men in that room on, especially Sam Decker. It was a relief to know that he would no longer have to.

Mateo Salvador paced. He had sent his wife back to Mexico until this mess was over. He loved her and was not about to allow Sam Decker to do to her as he had done to Decker's woman. He glanced out the patio door and could see the men and dogs patrolling the grounds. He had tripled his security in the past twenty-four hours, both at home and the office.

Deep down, part of him wondered if he should have followed Enchufe Rojo's earlier advice and just let everything drop after the killing of Kyle Mundy. Alas, it was water under the bridge now. Now it was war! Sam Decker would pay for coming into his house and striking him. That made it a matter of honor for El Toro. Sam Decker must die!

The Everglades, the isle of the Hidden Ones.

Mark Mundy tossed and turned in his bed. Beads of sweat had formed on his forehead, his hair plastering against it. His eyelids twitched as he was deep in REM sleep.

It was morning and he was full. Miss Lacy had made him a big breakfast with pancakes, bacon, and eggs and toast, and he had eaten it all, topping it off with a big glass of milk. Daddy had come to pick him up and Miss Lacy had walked them to the door. Mark had followed his daddy out to the car and climbed in, making sure to fasten his seatbelt. Then they had driven to the dock to wait on the ferry boat to come and take them back over to Duck Key.

Daddy had parked his car on the drive leading to the loading ramp. "Do you want to get out and watch the ferry as it comes across the water to the dock?" his daddy has asked. Of course, he did! That was a silly question. Mark loved everything about the water. He was a good swimmer and his daddy took him every chance that he got.

Mark was watching the boats out on the water when he felt his daddy grab his shoulder. Mark looked up. Daddy was drawing his gun. He looked down into Mark's eye's. "Run, Mark!" and he pushed him. Mark heard the shots as he darted away, glanced back and saw blood spraying from his daddy's body. Mark dived into the water. He went down deep and then started kicking back towards the surface. He climbed out and ducked down behind a piling, hanging to it for dear life. Then the police came. Chief Monica, Miss Nora, and they had called Miss Lacy.

Miss Lacy had been so nice to him. She had held him and comforted him. The Mr. Sam had taken him out and they had started building the stilt house. They had come back to bury Mark's Daddy.

The preacher had said words and then Mark had been given a folded-up flag to commemorate his father's time in the service. They were walking back to Mr. Sam's car when the monsters came. They had come in two cars and they had guns and *they started shooting. One man was firing a rifle at him and had missed. Then Miss Lacy grabbed him and was trying to get him to cover. He heard a loud booming sound, and then Miss Lacy fell on him, and he could feel a warm liquid dripping onto his face. Mark started to scream!*

"Mark, shh. It's okay, I'm here," Julia Sinclair said as she gathered the frightened ten-year old into her arms. She could only imagine what his nightmare had been about. So, she sat and comforted him, because for the moment, that was the best she could do.

CHAPTER SIX

Julia Sinclair gathered Mark Mundy into her arms, holding him tight and muttering calming words to the ten-year-old boy who had been stripped of everything that he held dear. She should call Sam, but that would wait until morning. Mark needed more help than she alone could give him. He needed to see a shrink. Someone who could help him get through the things he was feeling. In the morning, she would call Monica. Monica might be able to recommend someone.

Julia rocked Mark, whispering words of comfort to him. Soon he was back asleep, his breathing deep and steady. Julia eased him back onto his bed and covered him with the thin cotton sheet again. Hopefully he would sleep through the rest of the night without nightmares. She leaned back in her chair and closed her eyes, hoping that she would be able to grab some sleep herself.

Scorpion Cay, Florida Keys.

Police Chief Monica Sinclair had awakened early. The horizon was pink as the sun moved up into the pre-dawn sky. Bailey nosed her hip as Monica put coffee in a filter and put it into the coffee maker. "Knock it off, I'll feed you after I start my coffee," Monica told her. The Rottweiler-beagle cross walked over and laid down on the floor in a corner. Monica shook her head. She supposed that she should swing by Decker's boat and feed Elvis before the cat started terrorizing the rest of the marina.

Monica had never believed Decker about the cat's capabilities until she had seen Elvis in action. Elvis was everything that Sam had claimed, as well as being a very loving cat. He seemed to like her too. Monica was one of the few people besides Decker who could get close to him. Lacy could, and Mark, but other than them, only Sam and Monica. So, while Sam was off the Island pursuing his revenge on El Toro, that left Monica to care for the cat. It would have to be on the boat though. Bailey might make the mistake of being friendly and Elvis might well kill her dog.

Nora Santiago checked her phone as she made breakfast for her husband Juan and the kids. No calls from Rafe or from Sam. She had hoped to hear something. Maybe Sam had finally broken down and called Monica. She didn't think so, but she could at least hope.

Miami, Florida.

Sam Decker kept his eyes on the warehouse that was the central storage for El Toro's Flakka operation. Rafael was already out there, planting charges, as were Jake and Joe. It was time to hit El Toro where it would hurt the most, in the pocket book!

If they cut off his cash flow, it would hurt him. It would also turn his suppliers against him. That meant that El Toro would be fighting on two fronts instead of just one. That would further drain the drug lord's resources.

Decker liked that idea. He wanted to draw El Toro out into the light of day, expose him and his operations and make them public. Revealing him as the supplier of this dangerous drug and sway public opinion against him.

Flakka was a plague in South Florida. People strung out on the drug went insane, trying to kill and eat innocent bystanders. It was turning them into mindless zombies. Flakka was a major concern for law enforcement in the area.

The Everglades.

Hachi frowned as she watched the two cars pull into the parking lot. She had a bad feeling about them. They looked like the type that Joe had warned her might come around. She took a deep breath and let it out slowly as the first of the men entered. He was dark-skinned and had a Mexican accent.

"I want to rent a couple of airboats," he said.

"I can take care of that," Hachi nodded, acting as if nothing was wrong. She gave no indication that she had a 12-guage pump-shotgun under the counter with a load of double ought buck already chamber-loaded.

"I need two boats. Do you have any guides available?" he asked nonchalantly.

"I am afraid not. The owner is gone today, so I don't have any guides available."

"What about you?"

"I'm from Miami. I just work here," Hachi smiled.

"Okay. How much for two airboats?"

"Twenty bucks an hour or $100.00 bucks a day," Hachi smiled.

"Okay, here is two hundred bucks," he told her, dropping the cash on the counter.

"Sure thing, let me get the contracts," Hachi told them walking over to the file cabinets. She opened a drawer and pulled two boat contracts out of the drawer. She carried them back to the counter and had him sign them. Hachi handed him two sets of keys and then walked them out to the airboats. The men took the keys and took their places on the boats as the leaders fired the engines and then slowly moved away from the docks. Hachi watched them go. Once they had disappeared, she ran inside and grabbed the phone. She dialed Joe's cellphone!

"Hachi," Joe answered his phone.

"Joe, some bad men were just here. They rented two airboats and took off into the 'glades," Hachi explained.

"How do you know they were bad?"

"They gave me a bad vibe, so I stilled my mind and listened to the whispers of the swamp spirits. I think they are hunting for the island of the Hidden Ones."

"Then they will have a near impossible task. The Hidden Ones chose their island well. They also have guardians that watch over them."

"How well will those guardians fare against automatic weapons?"

"Better than you might think, Hachi. They have watched over that island from the time that the first of the Hidden Ones landed to make their home there. They guard them still. I will let Sam know. We may well be taking our war into the 'glades to spare innocent lives."

"I just thought that you would want to know."

"You did good to let me know, Hachi. Now tell the birds, so that they might spread the word, and then the creatures of the swamp will be watchful of these foolish men," Joe told her.

"Yes, master," Hachi said. She broke the connection. Joe was her teacher. He was a shaman, and she was his student, learning the old ways from him.

Hachi walked out onto the dock. A Pelican was sitting on one of the dock pilings. Hachi walked to the piling and looked into the Pelican's eyes. She cleared her mind. Then she pictured the faces of the men that had rented the boats. Moments later, the Pelican took off in flight, traveling to spread the word of the dangerous men in the swamp.

Miami, Florida.

"Sam," Joe spoke quietly from behind Decker, making him jump.

"Joe, what have I told you about doing that?" Sam gasped, trying to slow his heartbeat down. He had been sitting on a bench on the sidewalk where he could keep an eye on El Toro's office building, waiting for the drug lord to show.

"El Toro has sent men into the swamps. Hachi just called to let me know," Joe explained.

"Is Mark safe?"

"Mark is in no danger from them. The guardian spirits of the swamp will protect him."

"I hope you're right, Joe."

"Have faith, Sam," Joe replied.

"Right now, faith is something I don't have a lot of," Decker replied bitterly.

"Your pain is fresh, my friend. With time, it will hurt less, but it will never go completely away."

"So everybody tells me."

"There is no magic to help you grieve, my friend. You will do it as you must. Taking down this evil man will help."

"I hope so, Joe. I hope it will help Mark too."

"It will. How much longer will you wait here?" Joe asked.

"Until I know he is here. Then we will start hitting his people on the streets," Decker said.

"I will be ready."

Mateo Salvador glared out the window of his armored limousine. He hated being cooped up in the armored vehicle. He much preferred his convertible with the wind blowing in his hair. The convertible was a luxury that he could not afford, not with Sam Decker out there hunting him. So instead, he was forced into a gilded cage like an animal. His freedom nothing more than an illusion. *"Madre Dios!"* he yelled, slamming his fists down on the seat beside him.

"Everything okay, Jefe?" his driver asked regarding him in the rearview mirror.

"No, but it will be soon enough," El Toro replied. He had sent word back to Mexico and men were being sent to help him get rid of Sam Decker.

Decker used his binoculars to shoot video of El Toro arriving at his office. One driver and two bodyguards got out to escort their boss inside. Good. That meant that meant that he was taking

Decker seriously. Sam smiled. He didn't want El Toro's fall to be too easy. He planned on striking fear into his heart before he finally took him down and turned him over to the DEA for the murder of Kyle Mundy and Lacy Ryan.

Decker pulled out his phone and dialed Rafael. "He is in the office. Start the first part of operation hellfire." Decker hung up and walked away, heading for the rental car he had parked nearby.

"That Sam?" John Longfellow asked, looking over at Rafael Cortez.

"Yes. Time to get this show on the road."

"I figured," Longfellow said as he opened his door and stepped out of the car. It had taken a while for him to warm up to Cortez. They had worked on opposite sides of the law for a long time, but they had put that aside when Decker had been framed for the murder of his ex-wife by Russian gangsters.[2] While the Russians had committed the act, it was actually an old nemesis of Decker's that had been behind it. Working together, they had taken the guy down and cleared Sam's name.

Rafael climbed out of the car, slipping the sling of a Mossberg 500 Persuader shotgun over his shoulder. Together they started walking towards the warehouse that was twenty yards away, and on

---

[2] Decker P.I. Best Served Cold

the waterfront. Of course, in Miami, a lot of places were on the waterfront.

"Hang back a bit, I see a guard at the corner," Longfellow said, his hand slipping inside his windbreaker to draw his Smith & Wesson .41 Magnum from its holster. John walked, holding the weapon behind his leg and out of sight. He was two steps away before the guy spotted him and turned to face him. John pulled his gun up until the barrel was touching the tip of the man's nose. "Don't even breathe hard," he told the man. The guard blinked his understanding as Rafael moved around him and stripped him of his weapon. Plastic zip ties quickly secured his hands and duct tape served to gag him. John had him kneel and Rafael zip-tied his ankles together as well.

"Not a sound," Rafael told him, looking the man in the eye. The guard nodded in fright, not liking whatever he was seeing in the former Cuban enforcer's eyes.

"Let's move on," John whispered.

"Agreed," Rafe said as he stood. They moved towards the door leading inside the warehouse. So far, everything was running by the numbers, but both men knew that wouldn't last. Still, they would hope for the best and try to complete their mission. Rafael smiled, wondering out El Toro would react to having his main stash going up in smoke!

Andy Baca and Wally Norwood sat across from El Toro's home. They watched as the guards walked the grounds and two men stood at the gate, keeping an eye on passing traffic. "This is going to be fun," Wally said.

"For once, I agree with you. It will be nice to take these assholes down a peg or two," Jake drawled from the driver's seat.

"So, when do we make our play?"

"According to my watch and Sammy's plan, ten minutes," Jake replied. It had seemed fitting for the aging Texas Ranger and the former smuggler to team up for this part of the operation.

Chapter Seven

The Everglades.

Marco Silva looked around the expanse of swamp. So far, they had found no trace of the mysterious Isle of the Hidden Ones where Mark Mundy was being kept. He wasn't all that sure that Red Jack's information was all that accurate. Silva was part of the Cartel that El Toro fronted for in Miami. He was one of their head enforcers.

God it was hot out here in the swamp. The heat was very different from Mexico. More humidity. He took a bottle of water out of the styrofoam cooler and unscrewed the top. The water felt good going down. It cooled his insides.

The Everglades was an interesting place. He had seen a lot of wildlife. Alligators, salt-water crocodiles, even a couple of bullsharks in some of the deeper channels. And snakes. He had never seen so many goddam snakes in all of his life! Not even back in Mexico!

The swamp was alive, almost like a living organism all by itself. The passing of the airboats did not go unnoticed. Every denizen of the swamp knew exactly where the men were. Cold eyes kept track of their passage. Eyes that remained hidden and watching.

Scorpion Cay, Florida Keys.

Monica Sinclair opened the hatch and made her way down into *The Hunter,* Decker's boat. She could tell that Sam had cleaned the litter box before he left the island. That was something at least. "Mroow?" she heard Elvis before she saw him. The orange tabby was curled up on one of the bench seats in the galley, yellow eyes watching her.

"Hi, Elvis. I dropped by to feed you and give you some belly rubs," Monica told the cat. He blinked at her, and for some strange reason, she was sure that he had understood her. She paused to scratch his neck and ears for a couple of minutes before making her way to the plastic trashcan where Sam kept the cat food. She popped it open and used the ceramic cup inside to scoop up some kibble and poured it into his dish. Elvis jumped down and walked over as she added a second scoop. She put the cup back in the food bin and then got a bottle of water and poured it into his water dish.

Elvis munched on the fresh food for a couple of minutes before getting a drink and then rubbing against her legs. Moinica picked the cat up and stroked his fur as she settled into the bench seat and just held and petted him. Elvis purred loudly. After five minutes, Monica put him down. "I have to get to work, but I will be back tonight," she told the cat. Elvis purred loudly as she headed back up the steps. Monica secured the hatch and headed for her car.

Miami, Florida.

Flames and smoke erupted fromn the warehouse on the waterfront. The sounds of the explosions from inside were muffled by the rapidly disintegrating walls and support beams. Sam Decker smiled as he watched the roof collapse inward. There had been nearly a metric ton of Flakka inside the warehouse. Now it was gone. Decker glanced at his watch before climbing into his rental car and driving away, leaving the smoke, burning rubble behind.

Wally Norwood had concealed himself in some bushes outside El Toro's walled in compound. He had an M-79 grenade launcher, the famous 40mm 'bloop' gun, so called for the noise it made as the grenades were fired out of it. He had strung a line to the top of the wall that held a fiber optic camera lense in it that was giving him a live feed of what was going on inside the grounds of the compound. Jake Baca had a similar set-up on the other side of the grounds. Wally glanced away from the lap top screen and checked his watch. It was time.

Wally loaded the first of the High Explosive rounds into the launcher. He aimed into the sky over the wall and pulled the trigger. A gardener's shed and a car in the driveway both exploded in twin balls of fire. Wally reloaded and fired again. The assault on El Toro was on! Three minutes later, Wally was stowing his gear in his rental car and was making his way around the back to pick up Jake.

Sgt. Carl Lines shook his head as he walked the perimeter of the demolished warehouse. One of the responding uniforms walked up to him. "Nobody saw anything until it blew. Then they watched it fall," the patrolman said.

"Why am I not surprised," Lines shook his head. Lines was about six foot and built like a lineback, a position he had excelled at in college. He still worked out at the gym three times a week to maintain himself. He had a medium length hairstyle for a guy, parted on the right. Blond-haired and blue eyed, he could have easily passed as a surfer on the west coast. The skin around his eyes was lines and he looked tired.

"Hey Carl," Mick Gordon, his partner called.

"Have you got something, Mick?" Lines asked, taking his eyes off the rubble. The fire department was still hosing it down, no doubt washing away all kinds of forensic evidence.

"You'll never believe who owned this place," Gordon was grinning like the Chesire Cat.

"Who?" Lines asked, looking his partner in the eye.

"Mateo Salvador owns it through something called DeSilva Holding Company."

"Interesting."

"I thought so. Oh, and I just heard on the radio that units are rolling on Salvador's residence following reports from neighbors of loud explosions inside the wall."

"Maybe we should check it out."

"Maybe we should," Carl said, heading for the car.

"Are you ever going to tell why you hate this guy so much?" Gordon asked.

"Maybe. Maybe not," Lines said as he drove.

"I'll just go ahead and take that as a no. So what do you think is going on? Some kind of gang war?"

"I've got a bad feeling that it may be worse than that."

"Worse? Really? What could be worse?"

"Do you remember seeing the news about that DEA agent killed on Scorpion Cay a couple of weeks back and then the woman that was assassinated at his funeral?" Lines asked.

"Yeah, I remember reading about that," Gordon nodded.

"Well, the woman? She was Sam Decker's fiance."

"Well fuck me running," Gordon breathed.

"Exactly," Lines sighed. Gordon pulled out a pack of cigarettes and shook it free, put it in his mouth and lit it. He exhaled the smoke.

"You think Decker is behind this, and the explosions at Salvador's house?"

"You don't?"

"Well shit."

Mateo Salvador was on a call when Luis Carnicino rushed into his office. "Bentley, let me call you back, it appears that some sort of emergency has come up," he told the caller before hanging up the telephone. "What is it, Luis?"

"The warehouse is gone. Somebody blew it up, brought the whole place crashing down. Alex called and said that somebody was lobbing grenades at the house as well," Luis said, speaking rapidly. He was concerned.

"Have the car brought around. I need to see this for myself."

"Are you sure that is a good idea? What is if this is just something to draw you out into the open where Decker can shoot you down?"

I don't think Decker would do that. If he wanted me dead, he could have killed me the night he broke into my house," El Toro said.

"You told me yourself that he said that was a warning," Luis reminded him.

"Sam Decker wants to hurt me, to make me suffer for what I did to him and the boy. Was anyone killed at the warehouse or my home?" El Toro asked.

"No. Nobody was even injured unless you count having the shit scared out of them."

"Fine. I will stay here. Get me Enchufe Rojo. It is time to put this Decker business behind me, once and for all," El Toro said.

The assassin known as Red Jack sat at a table outside a bodega in Little Havana. He was meeting someone. A cop. One that had some very valuable information. Sunglasses covered his eyes as he leaned back in his seat, pretending to read the Miami Herald as his eyes scanned the street. Then he spotted the man that he was waiting on. Red Jack laid the newspaper on the table in front of him and the man in the ill-fitting suit dropped into the chair across from him.

"Jack, it's been a while," the man said.

"Yes, it has Hank. Too long."

"The Public Safety Director has agreed to look the other way on this. He's giving Decker and his people carte blanche on this. As long as no innocents get involved, they have a free hand to take El Toro out," Hank Marsetti told him.

"Why?" Red Jack asked.

"Because the DOJ is backing Decker's play. The Feds have decided that using Decker to send a message about what happens when you target the DEA is the best way to go. And with Decker being a civilian, they have deniability," Marsetti shrugged.

"How high does this go?" Red Jack asked.

"High up in Justice, maybe even all the way to the oval office. Flakka has been labeled the most dangerous drug to ever reach American shores. A scourge, even. Far more dangerous than Coke or Heroin," Marsetti looked away.

"That is very interesting news."

"I thought so. Are we good?"

"We are," Red Jack said; drawing and envelope from his windbreaker and sliding it across the table. Marsetti made the envelope disappear.

"See you around," the informant said, standing and walking away. Red Jack picked up his beer and drained it. His cell phone picked that moment to ring. Red Jack pulled it out and looked at the screen, and then he answered it.

"He wants you to come in."

"When?"

"Right now, there have been a couple of events. He requires your presence," Luis said.

"I am on my way," Red Jack replied.

"So, what is next?" Joe looked at Sam.

"El Toro has a boat. I want to sink it," Decker said.

"What kind of boat?" Jake Baca asked.

"Well, actually it is a 35-million-dollar yacht."

"So, a big boat?"

"You could call it that," Sam grinned.

"You are trying to make him come after you," Rafael said, finally understanding.

"You've got it."

"Why would he do that?" Jake looked puzzled.

"Because it makes anything Sam does self-defense," Wally inserted.

"I thought you wanted to have him arrested?" John Longfellow looked at Decker accusingly.

"I do, but I want the case against him to be air-tight. I don't want some fast-talking lawyer to get him off," Decker replied.

"You are one scary man, Sam," Jake Baca said.

"I learned from the best," Decker replied glancing at Wally. The Country Music Icon and Texas Ranger returned his smile with a twinkle in his eye.

"Yes, you did," Wally acknowledged.

"You people scare me," Longfellow sighed.

"You've just forgotten how to have fun, Johnny," Wally told him.

"You call this fun?" Longfellow asked.

"You don't?"

"Wally."

"Let it go, John. All of you are doing this for me, and for Lacy. I want to draw El Toro into the everglades. That way we don't have to worry about innocents getting in the way," Decker told him.

CHAPTER EIGHT

Scorpion Cay, Florida Keys.

Monica Sinclair answered her telephone in her office. "Scorpion Cay, P.D., Chief Sinclair speaking," she said.

"How is Elvis?" Sam Decker's voice asked.

"He misses you. And according to the call I got from Julia earlier, Elvis isn't the only one," Monica replied.

"I know. I plan on making a trip to the island in the next day or so," Decker replied.

"You need to call Julia direct, take a few minutes to reassure Mark that you are okay."

"Okay, I can do that. Thank you for taking care of Elvis for me until this is over."

"He's a good kitty. Besides, I'd be afraid of getting on his bad side," Monica said, shaking her head because it was the truth.

"Tell me about it. He's probably going to be very cranky when Mark and I get back," Decker chuckled.

"Glad to hear you're planning on coming back. For a while there I wasn't so sure."

"I wouldn't do that to Mark. He's been through enough."

"I glad to hear that, Sam. You don't know how glad."

"I do, Monica, trust me. Nora told Rafael you wanted me to call."

"They were right. From watching the news, you've been busy up in Miami."

"It is going to get a lot busier before it is over."

"I figured. Be careful Sam, both for you and Mark."

"I will, Monica. I promise," Decker told her before hanging up. Monica put the receiver back in the cradle and looked at the clock. It was getting about time to go give Elvis his evening meal.

Nora Santiago frowned as she drove her unmarked car through the marina parkinglot. There were a couple of unfamiliar faces sitting on a bench where they had a good view of Decker's boat, *The Hunter.* It gave her an uneasy feeling. This wasn't something to put out over the radio. She pulled out her cell phone and dialed Monica.

Her boss answered on the first ring. "Sinclair."

"Get down to the marina as quick as you can. There are a couple of strange faces down here and they appear to be keeping an eye on Sam's boat," Nora explained.

"I'm on my way. Have they seen you?" Monica asked.

"No, I pulled into one of the ferry parking slots. I can see them, but they have no idea who I am and they don't seem to have noticed me."

"Then sit tight and keep an eye on them until I get there. I'm going to have Rufus roll a couple of additional cars to the marina just to be on the safe side. If these guys are working for the man that ordered Lacy's death, I want them in the worst possible way."

"Copy that," Nora replied, breaking the connection. She brought up the camera on her phone and zoomed in on the two men, getting some good video of their faces. They looked bored. Nora knew that wasn't going to last. Once Monica got to the marina, things were going to get lively real quick!

Miami, Florida.

Sam Decker had put on a gray tropical white suit over a light gray shirt and charcoal gray tie. His shoes were black and polished to a high sheen. Dark sunglasses covered his eyes, concealing his face to some degree. He carried a briefcase in his left hand. He had a Ruger LC9 9mm tucked in his waistband behind his right kidney.

The gun was loaded with 9mm 115-grain jacketed hollow-point ammunition. It seemed like overkill for the Miami Palms Yacht Club, but things were never what they seemed. Mateo Salvador had a hundred foot yacht moored there. Decker wanted to get aboard and prepare a little surprise for El Toro.

He looked like he belonged, like an attorney on their way to speak to a privilaged client. It was a form of role cameoflage. Half of penetrating an enemies location was looking like you belonged. El Toro wasn't on the yacht, which meant that it wouldn't have as much heavy security as his house did.

As far as its owner was concerned, the yacht was a status symbol and expensive toy. It was a symbol of his ill-gotten gains. Decker was about to exploit that in a *very* public fashion. Rafael was keeping watch for him in the parking lot.

Decker stopped next to where the expensive boat was moored. There was no one in sight. Decker stepped onto the boat and waited for a long moment. Nobody appeared, which indicated that there likely was no one on board. That was good news, at least for him. Not so much for Mateo Salvador. Decker knelt next to the door that lead below deck. He pulled out his set of lockpicks and was inside in less than a minute.

El Toro was furious. He had lost nearly a ton of product, a car, several outbuildings, and half of his staff. They had quit after the assault on his home. It made him look weak, the fact that he couldn't defend his own home against Sam Decker! That had to change! He sent more men out to look for the private investigator. More eyes on the street were bound to find the man, as well as anyone working with him!

Enrico Cuzco yelped as a big hand closed around the back of his neck and he was lifted into the air. "What the hell?" he sputtered as a face appeared in front of him.

"I want all of your Flakka," the stoic giant holding him said softly. Just the tone made him shiver.

"Okay, I'll show you where I keep my stash," Enrico stuttered.

"Good," the big Indian told him.

"This is getting old fast," Jake Baca said. He was on his second bottle of water as he and Wally followed two of El Toro's dealers.

"Maybe so, Jake, but it is helping Sam," Wally told him.

"I know, Wally. I was just hoping for a little more action."

"I know Jake. We'll get our chance. Right now, Sam is wanting to piss El Toro off. He wants to goad him into coming after him, full bore."

"I know, but I am really wanting to shoot someone," Jake groused.

"You aren't the only one, Jake. I am too," Wally replied.

Decker opened the briefcase and removed several blocks of Semtex from it. He placed one, complete with detonator in the engine room, and spread several others out around the boat. He had an electronic detonator ready to go for when the time was right. Decker left the boat and headed for his rental car.

Once Decker reached his car, he scanned the waters of the Marina, making sure that there was nobody that could be harmed. He slipped inside his car and triggered the remote detonator. The yacht seemed to lift three feet above the water, and landed with a huge splash. It also began to sink immediately. Decker found himself grinning as he put the car in gear and headed back to the hotel.

El Toro had already been pissed before, but this should be enough to drive him over the edge. One thing Decker had learned a long time ago. If you could make an opponent so angry that they weren't thinking straight, it would make them make mistakes. Mistakes that could make taking them out all the easier. Decker wanted El Toro livid, so angry that he couldn't see straight. He wanted the man to pull out all the stops in coming after him.

Scorpion Cay, Florida Keys.

"Are they still there?" Monica asked when she had Nora back on the line. Except this time, it was on her cell phone and she was pulling in to the marina parking lot.

"They are. They look like they are getting ready to approach the boat," Nora told her.

"Do they appear to be armed?" Monica asked.

"If they are, it is handguns. One of them does have a duffle that might have heavier ordnance inside it. It looks like it's got some weight too it."

"Dammit, that might be a bomb of some kind. Otherwise I'd let them break in so Elvis could get some exercise."

"Monica! That cat is dangerous!"

"Only to people that break in to Sam's boat," Monica replied as she parked her car and slipped outside. She grabbed the Mossberg 500 12-guage out of the car. She knew that the tubular magazine had 8 rounds in it. Holding the shotgun in her right hand, muzzle towards the ground, she walked towards Decker's boat. "Wait until I'm a little bit closer."

"Sure thing, Boss," Nora replied.

Monica stayed low as she made her approach. She hung up her cell phone and slipped it back into her pants pocket. She pulled the shotgun up to port-arms position and flicked off the safety with her thumb. Once she jacked that first round into the chamber, she had a feeling she would be shooting as fast as she could pull the trigger and pump in fresh rounds.

Motion to her right caught her eye and she looked over at Nora. Monica nodded her readiness. They stepped out as the men reached the edge of the dock. "Police, stop right there!" Monica yelled, working the pump on the 12-guage. The two men spun towards them, guns in their hands. Monica fired at the same time as Nora. The guy with the bag dived away rolling along the dock as Monica worked the pump again, jacking a fresh round of buckshot into the chamber. The man fired at them as Monica squeezed the trigger and the shotgun bucked in her fists. The man fell back on the dock as several crimson flowers blossomed on his chest.

"Nora, you okay?" Monica asked.

"Not really. The bastard shot me," Nora was slumped against a car, her left sleeve red with blood. Monica got on the radio and called for a bus and the medical examiner.

The Everglades, Island of the Hidden Ones.

"Do you want to talk about it?" Julia
Sinclair asked as she sat down next to Mark Mundy.

"Talk about what?" he asked guardedly. He
refused to meet her eyes.

"About the nightmares," Julia said softly.

"What nightmares? Those are for babies,"
Mark said defiantly as he looked away.

"Everybody had nightmares, Mark. Nobody
is immune to them."

"Well, I don't have them," he said angrily.

"Do you remember me being there last
night?" Julia asked softly. Other kids were playing,
but they were far enough away that they couldn't
hear anything that Julia and Mark said to each other.

"Yes, I remember," Mark admitted.

"I sat there all night because I know you
have been having nightmares Mark. Sometimes I
have them too."

"I was being chased by monsters with guns.
They wanted to kill me."

"How did that make you feel?"

"It made me scared."

"It should have, Mark. When men chase
you with guns, it is a very scary thing."

"Have men with guns ever chased you?"
Mark looked into her eyes. Julia considered her
answer and then decided to tell him the truth.

"Yes, they have. Sam Decker saved my
life," Julia told him.

"Daddy and Miss Lacy both said that Mr. Sam was good at helping people."

"He is, Mark. That's one of the reasons that he sent you here. So, that you would be safe from the men with guns."

"But what if something happens to Mr. Sam?" Mark asked, a tear started to drip down his cheek.

"Nothing is going to happen to Sam, Mark. He is just too good at what he does," Julia smiled.

"I hope you're right, Miss Julia. Mr. Sam is all I have left," Mark told her.

"You've got me as well Mark. You also have Joe, Wally, Monica, and Nora. You have a lot of people that care about you," Julia told him.

"I guess."

"Trust me, Mark. You do. I have a friend that I am going to have come and talk to you as well. She is really good at helping people sort out their feelings about things," Julia told him.

CHAPTER NINE

Miami, Florida.

"Okay, it looks like we found another distribution center," Jake Baca said.

"Yes it does," Wally nodded.

"What are we going to do about it?" Jake looked over at him.

"We are finally going to do what you wanted to do earlier," Wally grinned.

"What's that?" Jake asked.

"Shoot some bad guys."

"It is about damn time," Baca grinned.

You've gotten bloodthirsty in your old age, Jake," Wally told him.

"No, I just have little tolerence for assholes that sell this poison," Jake replied.

"I knew that there was something about you that I liked," Wally grinned. They climbed out of the car and Wally drew out a pump-shotgun with a pistol grip and extended magazine that held 8-rounds plus on in the chamber for a total load of nine.

"Sure," Jake Baca replied, pulling out his old Colt 1911-A .45. Together they walked up to the doorway. "You want to do the honors?" Jake asked.

"Feel free. You've been waiting to open this dance," Wally shrugged.

"Yes I have," Jake grinned as he turned the knob and opened the door. They stepped into the house. Four men were sitting at a table, bagging up stuff that looked like aquarium gravel from a five gallon pickel bucket. "You boys need to drop your guns and get out," Jake told them.

"Like hell," one of the man snarled, reaching for the gun tucked into his waistband. Jake fired and the man's head blew apart, blood and brain matter splattered the faces of the other men. They started to scramble for cover while drawing their weapons. The shotgun in Wally's hands roared into the confrontation, taking down another man.

A bullet ripped past Jake's head as he fired again. Jake took the shooter down with a well-placed round as buckshot took the last man's head off. "That was intense," Jake said, his ears ringing.

"That it was," Wally replied, jacking a fresh round into the chamber of his shotgun. He reached down and pulled out a road flare, twisted off the top

and scraped it to life. Red fire lanced from the end.
Wally tossed it into the bucket of Flakka and
grinned as the drugs started to melt. He looked at
Jake. "Time to go," he said.

Moving quickly, they walked out to the
rental car and got in and drove away. Police and
fired would be called soon enough.

"My yacht?" El Toro screamed at the top of
his lungs into the cell phone that he had pressed to
his ear.

"Gone. Several street level dealers have
been robbed, their supplies destroyed, and another
of your stash houses was burned to the ground,"
Antonio Ribero explained to his boss. He hated
being the bearer of bad news.

"Find Sam Decker!" El Toro snarled,
snapping his phone closed.
El Toro threw the glass of wine he had been holding
against the wall. Wine spashed down on the carpet,
staining it. El Toro was in a rage! He flipped his
desk over and picked up a lamp, smashing it into a
wall as well.

He stood in the center of his home office, his
body shaking with rage. He took in several deepo
breathes and let them out slowly, working to calm
himself. Sam Decker was responsible for what was
happening. He was sure of that. He had to find
Decker and kill him!

"From what we could see and hear, El Toro is going crazy with rage," Rafael Cortez said.

"Do you agree with that, John?" Sam Decker asked.

"I do. I think that he is ready to come after you, Sam," John Longfellow agreed.

"Joe, I think we need to move into the swamp. The stilthouse would make a good base to operate from if we can draw him into the Everglades," Decker said.

"It would. You must remember, he already has men searching the everglades for you or for Mark," Joe reminded him.

"I know that. I'm just about ready to let them find me," Decker said. Somehow, his smile didn't quite reach his eyes.

"So long as you remember that we are not the only ones out there."

"I know that Joe. There are a lot of folks who live in the swamp, not just the Hidden Ones. Most of them won't like El Toro's people any better than we do."

"Agreed," Joe said.

Everglades, Island of the Hidden Ones.

"Miss Julia?" Mark asked.

"Yes, Mark?" she looked at him.

"Thank you for staying with me."

"I like staying with you, Mark."

"Do you really?" he asked, looking at her anxiously.

"I do, Mark. You are a good boy. You've just been through a lot," Julia told him.

"I wish Mr. Sam would call or come by."

"I know you do, Mark. I am sure Sam will come by as soon as he can."

"I heard some noises tonight. Strange sounds that seemed to drift across the water. They made me feel a little scared."

"You heard the guardians talking," Julia told him.

"The Guardians?" Mark asked.

"The Hidden Ones made a pact with the guardians way back when they first came to this island. The guardians have lived in the Everglades as long as they have been. Many of the tribes feared them and sought to drive them off. But the Hidden Ones made friends with them, and offered them sacrifices for their protection. The guardians now watch over the Hidden Ones and protect them from those who would come to do harm to the colony," Julia explained.

"But what are the Guardians?" Mark asked.

"Some folks call them skunk apes. Others call them sasquatch or big foot. The thing that is most important to remember is that they watch over this island and protect everyone here from outsiders," Julia explained.

"Will they protect me?" Mark asked, looking into her eyes.

"They will, because now you are a part of the Hidden Ones," Julia told him.

Scorpion Cay, Florida Keys.

"Who do you work for?" Monica Sinclair demanded. The surviving gunman looked up at her, his face expressionless. This was the man that Nora had winged as he had shot her. Nora was still in surgery. Monica had dragged this son of a bitch onto Decker's boat and stood over him.

"You don't think that you'll tell me everything that I want to know?" Monica asked him. The asshole yawned. "You'll be begging to talk to me very soon," Monica smiled. "Do you want to know why?"

"You can't torture me. You're a cop." He smirked at her. Men that smirked really annoyed her.

"You are right about that. What I can do, however, is shove you below deck and let the boat owner's home defense solution take care of you. You were breaking in after all," Monica smiled sweetly.

"Big deal."

"It's a bigger deal than you might think. A couple of other guys broke into this boat once. One never made it off. Not alive anyway. The other one, well he wasn't a pretty sight to look at, ever after the plastic surgery. You see that little sign on the wheelhouse? Right next to the hatch?" Monica asked.

"Yeah, what of it?" the crook asked.

"Read it. If you can read that is," Monica told him.

"This boat is protected by Kelso's Killer Cat protection system. Enter at your own risk. Kelso's Killer Cats? Never heard of it," he snorted.

"That really is too bad for you. It is time for you to meet Elvis," Monica told him.

"Elvis? Is that supposed to scare me? A cat named Elvis?"

Monica opened the hatch. "Walk down those steps and find out."

"You're kidding me, right?"

Monica drew her Glock. "Nope. Down the steps. Elvis, protect!" Monica called, closing the hatch behind him. For a moment there was silence. Then she heard a frightening yowl and the man began to scream, accompanied by a lot of thumping and hissing. Monica eased the hatch open and called to Elvis. "Release!" She stepped down the stairs and hit the lights.

The crook was backed up against the wall in a near fetal position, blood dripping from multiple scratches on his face and hands, his hair nearly standing on end. Elvis, Sam Decker's yellow tabby sat nearby, watching the man with yellow eyes. The cat licked his lips and the guy tried to become part of the bulkhead.

"So, are you ready to talk or do I go back out on deck and close the hatch again?" Monica asked.

"I'll talk, just keep that monster away from me," the man begged.

"So, who do you work for?" Monica asked again.

The Everglades.

Marco Silva sprayed more Deep Woods Off on his skin. The mosquitoes out here were beyond a nuisence. The damn bugs were doing their damndest to eat him and his men alive, despite the repellent! The guy at the store swore that it was the best that there was, but out here, it didn't seem all that effective.

The sun was starting to sink into the west and they were no damn closer to finding the kid than when they had started out that morning. El Toro was not going to be happy with them. There was nothing that Marco could do about that. He called over to Pablo who was driving the airboat. "Head back in. We'll come out again tomorrow."

Pablo nodded and plifted a walkie talkie to his mouth, transmitting the order to the crew of the other boat. There was a lot of distance to cover. The Everglades actually took up the major part of the state of Florida. The Everglades is a large region of freshwater marsh land that originally extended from Lake Okeechobee south to the tip of peninsular Florida. Once covering an area of 4,000 square miles (10,360 square km), the Everglades has been significantly reduced to less than half that size. The "sheet flow" of water across the land makes this area unique in contrast to other wetlands that typically rely on waters originating from rivers and streams.

It was still a lot of area to cover to find one hidden island deep in its heart. Marco hoped that El Toro realized that. Because it was certainly going to take more than a couple of days to locate that specific island that didn't appear on any maps of the region.

"Madre Dios!" one of the men yelled, pointing. Marco followed the direction of the man's arm. There was a huge creature standing on a small island that they were passing. It was covered in thick, stringy brown hair. It roared defiantly and ripped a small tree from the ground, throwing it after them!

The tree hit the water beside them with a mighty splash, and then they were past it, leaving the island behind. Marco shivered. He had heard tales of the skunk apes, the Florida equivalent of Big Foot. But he had never believed the stories until now!

Hachi had locked up the Quonset hut and taken up a watch inside the everglades near to her uncle's business. She watched to make sure that the men returned the two airboats. She didn't trust them, so she didn't want to be trapped within the structure of the building when they returned. So, she sat in a canoe in the mangroves where she could watch them, a 12-guage shotgun across her knees.

Death was coming to the Everglades. She could feel it. But who's death? Would it be her own? Or someone else's death? Hachi felt that it would likely be the death of others, possibly even the men that had rented the airboats.

She could hear the engines approaching. Sound tended to carry over the water, especially at night. Her thumb eased the safety on the shotgun to the off position. She wanted to be ready just in case the men came looking for her. The two airboats swung into the dock, and the men scrambled off them, making the lines fast. They walked to their cars and got in and drove off. Hachi gave a sigh of relief.

Chapter Ten

Miami, Florida.

Wally Norwood grimmaced as he looked at his phone to see who was calling. It was the Miami-Dade Police Director. "Hey Juan," Wally said.

"Your boy Decker has been pretty active Wally," Juan Perez said.

"He has. So far not one civilian has been hurt," Wally reminded him.

"So far. How much longer is this going to go on?"

"Not a day longer. Sam is moving out into the everglades. He is trying to entice El Toro and his men to follow him."

"Do you think they will?"

"They will. It is personal now for El Toro. He has to find and kill Sammy one way or another," Wally explained.

"Just don't let it happen in my city, Wally."

"I won't, Juan. I gave you my word on that," Wally told him.

"I wish I could believe you, Wally," Juan sighed.

"Do you really have a choice?"

"Not as much as I would like."

The thing about setting a trap for someone is all in getting them to take the bait. First, you have to make it so attractive that they cannot resist it. Then you have to make them really want it. You have to make them want it so bad that they would do anything to go after said bait. Which was exactgly what Decker and his friends were doing to El Toro.

In just a few strikes, they had wiped out most of his drug supply. The supply that he would sell to buy more from his supplier. Without any money, Mateo Salvador couldn't buy more Flakka, at least not without dipping into his personal accounts which were already under scrutiny by the DEA, the FBI, and the DOJ. As soon as he made any kind of sizable withdrawl from his accounts, the Feds would be looking up his ass with a microscope!

So, Mateo Salvador had no choice but to go after Sam Decker and eliminate him once and for all. Sam Decker smiled to himself. If everything worked out like he had planned, El Toro would come after him out in the swamp. If he did, Decker would take him down for Lacy's death, one way or another.

Decker returned his rental car and Joe picked him up in his ancient and rusting 1963 Chevrolete C-10 pick-up truck. Joe headed for the Everglades and the metal quonset hut that he ran his airboat and bait business out of. The others would follow.

"Hachi called again," Joe said.

"What did your neice have to say?" Sam asked.

"The men returned the boats, but they were talking about being attacked by a hairy beast out in the glades," Joe replied.

"You're telling me they saw a skunk ape? I thought those were just tall tales."

"All legends are based in facts, my friend."

"Are you actually telling me that you believe in the Florida version of Bigfoot?"

"What I believe doesn't matter. Those men hunting for the island saw something, and what they saw terrified them."

"What do you know about the Skunk Apes, Joe?"

"They serve as guardians for the island of the Hidden Ones. A pact was made from the time that the island was settled."

"What you are telling me is that Mark is being guarded by Bigfoot?"

"How can I tell you what you don't wish to believe? You refuse to accept that I can walk in the space between our world and the spirit world, even when you have witnessed it with your own eyes."

"El Toro looks like he is shitting all over himself," Jake Baca said as he watched the house through the binoculars.

"That's good to know," Wally grinned.

"He's spent the past hour yelling into his phone."

"He's not quite ready yet, but he will be once we get done. Johnny and Rafael are making sure of that right night now."

"What about Sam and Joe?"

"They are already on their way out to the island. Of course they did stop at a friends to pick up a few things that will prove helpful."

"Superior firepower is an awesome thing," Jake grinned.

"Yes it is," Wally smiled back.

"What are you thinking? Are we actually doing any good out here?" Longfellow asked.

"Are you always this cheerful, John?" Rafael asked, never taking his eyes off the rifle scope in front of him.

"I am when I am not 100% sure that I am doing the right thing."

"Maybe you shouldn't be here then."

"Maybe not. However, I am. So what should I say?"

"Go ahead and say what is on your mind," Rafael replied.

"I owe Sam. But I don't want to kill an innocent person," Longfellow sighed.

"Mateo Salvador is anything but innocent," Rafe said.

"I know that too," Longfellow sighed.

"What you need to ask yourself, John, is Salvador more innocent than Lacy or Kyle Mundy was?" Rafe told him.

"We both know that he's not."

"Then what the hell is your problem?"

"I don't know."

The Everglades.

Hachi had paddled to the small island where she made her home. The moon was rising in the sky by the time she reached it. The nightbirds sang their songs, just as did the crickets and the bullfrogs. She tied the line from the canoe to a mangrove tree near the sand beach. Her house was on stilts so she didn't have to worry about alligators or crocs. Snakes, however, were another matter. So, once she had climbed up into her home, she made a quick and detailed inspection to make sure that she hadn't received any slinky visitors while she was gone.

More and more alien species were encroaching on the everglades, all due to people dumping them once they had gotten too large for them to keep and maintain. Pythons, boa constricters, komodo dragons. Far too many apex predators that were eliminating the competion in the circle of life. Hachi kept her shotgun at ready as she prepared for best. She secured her doors and windows and turned off the lights. She settled into her bed and went to sleep.

Julia had tucked Mark in and waited until he had gone to sleep. She needed to walk, to clear her head. So, she moved to one of the paths that circled the island of the Hidden Ones. She was worried about Mark. He had seen too much, experienced too much for a child his age.

His mother had died of cancer. His father had been shot down in front of him. He had watched his surrogate mother die at his father's funeral. That was a hell of a lot for a kid to process. Maybe too much.

She had called Jessica Harmon down on Key West. Jessica was a specialist in Post-Traumatic Stress Syndrome. Julia had a feeling that she would be the perfect person to work with Mark. Jessica had agreed to come up to meet with Mark. Julia pulled out her cell phone and dialed Sam Decker.

"Julia, is Mark okay?" Decker asked when he answered.

"Physically, he's fine. I got ahold of Dr. Harmon in Key West. She's going to take the ferry to Marcos Island. Do you have somebody that can pick her up and bring her to see Mark?" Julia asked.

"I'm sure that Joe can make arrangements. Thank you, Julia. That was something I had been meaning to do but just hadn't been able to get to it yet."

"You've been busy."

"I'll try to get over to see Mark very soon. I promise," Decker sighed.

"I hope so, Sam. That boy needs you now more than ever," Julia told him. Julia ended the call and headed back to the small cabin that she and Mark were sharing. She had decided that bunking with her would make him feel less alone.

She smiled at how much her life had changed over the past three years. From jet-set fashion model to teaching a hidden tribe of Seminole children on a hidden island deep in the everglades. And she had never been happier in her life.

Miami, Florida.

"Any luck out there today?" Red Jack asked.

"We found a shit-load of mosquitoes and alligators and fucking snakes, but no hidden island. There are a lot of damn squatters out there that couldn't make it in the city. They just camp out on islands no bigger than sand-spits. There were a few small huts cobbled together from scrap wood, but nothing that looked like a settlement," Silva reported.

"It is a big territory. My informant is pretty sure that Decker sent the boy to a hidden colony of Seminole Indians somewhere out there in the 'Glades," Red Jack mused.

"There was a girl at that airboat place. She looked like an Indian. She might know where the island is at," Marco said.

You should probably talk to her and find out, Marco," Red Jack said.

"Me and the boys will do just that, Jefe. First thing in the morning," Silva replied with a wicked grin.

"Good. Now I have to see if anyone has managed to get a location on Decker. El Toro wants his head on a spike," Red Jack said. Marco got the message and stood to leave.

"I'll call as soon as I know something," Silva said, heading for the door. Red Jack nodded absently as he pulled out his cell phone and dialed another number.

Rafe was watching El Toro's place as former Deputy Marshal Longfellow slept in the passenger seat. There had been a lot of traffic rolling in and out all evening. It looked like El Toro had called in reinforcements, which likely meant that he was getting ready to chase Sam Decker into the everglades.

That was something, but it worried him. They were six against an army of killers. Even given they had the home ground, it was going to be a close thing. He wished he knew more about what Sam had planned for when they drew El Toro into the everglades after them.

So far, all he knew was that Sam planned to use the stilt house that they were building with Mark as a base of operations. Most swamps didn't bother him, because he knew what to expect. The everglades, however was changing. Too many foreign species had been being dumped there for years. Giant pythons, boas, even a few anacondas had been turned loose in the 'glades. All of them apex predators that contended with alligators and crocodiles, and freshwater sharks, bears, and panthers.

In the everglades, you never knew exactly what you might come face to face with. Rafael shook his head. He and the others would have to do what they could and hope that Mother Nature would lend them a hand with the rest.

El Toro, aka Mateo Salvador sat in his study, smoking a fat Cuban cigar. Alejandro was passing out sleeping arrangements and making sure all of his soldiers were fed. In the morning, after everyone had eaten, they would strike out into the everglades in search of the permanent thorn in his side! Sam Decker.

"Boss?" Angel Hermosa said from the doorway.

"What is it, Angel?" Salvador asked.

"Another ten stash houses have been hit. All of the Flakka we had is gone," Angel said, fear creeping into his voice. He knew what El Toro's temper could be like with messengers who delivered bad news.

"Decker! He is behind this! In the morning, we take the fight to him. Ernesto and another saw him and his big Indio friend heading into the everglades tonight. Come daylight, we will be going in after him. I don't care if the swamp water runs red with blood, Sam Decker will die!" El Toro shouted.

"Yes, Jefe," Angel said before ducking out. He hoped that his boss was right. For himself, Angel had a very bad feeling about the way things were going.

The Everglades.

Sam and Joe loaded three heavily laden duffels onto to one of the airboats after Joe made sure that it was fully gassed and ready for travel. He had left a note for Hachi, explaining that he and Decker were going out into the swamp and the others would be joining them the following day.

Sam took a seat up front, and Joe climbed into the driver's seat and fired the engine. With an expert hand, Joe guided the boat away from the dock and sent it shooting out into the night. Joe knew the 'glades like the back of his hand. They were his home, and he could find his way, even in total darkness.

Chapter Eleven

The moon was climbing into the night sky and out away from the city, the velvet blackness was coated with bright white stars. Even over the roar of the airboat's engine, Decker felt at peace as the night air whipped past his face. The everglades at time seemed like an entirely different world, almost prehistoric in its beauty. The alligators were certainly a reminder of that, given that they were thought to be the last remaining descents of the dinosaurs.

They traveled for an hour before Joe shut off the engine and guided the boat up onto the small beach that surrounded the island where Decker and the others were constructing the stilt house. It was a long way from being done, but it would provide them with a place to sleep and a base of operations in the coming days.

Decker pulled out his tactical light and made sure that there were no slithery surprises between the boat and the stilt house as he and Joe carried their duffels full of weapons and supplies. Wally would bring more when he and Jake came out tomorrow.

No snakes or spiders had made their way in during their absence. Same lit one of the hurricane lamps as Joe tossed up the bags. The sleeping bags were still in place, tightly rolled and sealed in plastic to keep out insect intruders. Decker cut the plastic and unrolled the two bags. He had slathered himself in insect repellent earlier and now lit some citronella candles to help keep the mosquitoes at bay. Finally, after they both had a cold beer, Decker and Joe crawled into the sleeping bags and went to sleep.

Mark Mundy tossed and turned in his sleep. The monsters had come back and were after him. He would run and hide but they kept finding him and he would escape and run some more.

It was hot and dark. Thick fog hung around him everywhere. He could hear them coming for him. He could hear the horrible thump of their footfalls as they chased him. He tripped over a tree branch and fell to the ground, his palms hit the mud and skidded forwards. Mark pushed to his feet. He

*could hear the loud explosions of gunshots, could
hear the snap of bullets tearing through the air
above his head. He could see the water. Mark
jumped in, not caring what sort of horrors might be
lurking beneath the calm surface!*

Mark woke up, screaming. The sound
snapped Julia awake and she moved instantly to the
other bed and slipped her arms around Mark. "I'm
here, Mark. I'm here," she whispered, doing
everything in her power to comfort the boy. She
could feel his tiny body shaking against her as he
was wracked with sobs.

Miami, Florida.

Red Jack tried to sleep, but he couldn't. He
was too wired up over the events of the day. El
Toro was almost out of control now, totally enraged
by the actions of Sam Decker and his friends.

They had in just a few days, crippled El
Toro's criminal empire to the very brink of
destruction. It continued to amaze Red Jack that
they had done so without inflicting harm on a single
innocent soul.

Finally, he could take it no more and threw
the covers off of him. Red Jack stood and headed
out of the bed room. In the living room, he poured
himself three fingers of whiskey and added two ice
cubes to it. He took a sip and reveled in the way it
felt as it burned its way down to his stomach.

Right now, El Toro was far more dangerous
to the cartels than his enemies were. He could have

to contact Alvarez and see what he wanted to do with El Toro. Alvarez would have answers. Red Jack took another drink of the whiskey. The burn felt good as it spread through his body. The alcohol was relaxing him. Red Jack tossed back the rest of what was in the glass, setting it on the night stand. He lay back on the bed and pulled the covers up over him. He closed his eyes, and was soon sleeping soundly.

Morning.

Mateo Salvador opened his eyes. He felt invigorated. He showered and dressed, not in a suit as he normally would, but in camouflage fatigues and combat boots. They were actually hunting clothes, but they felt more like an army uniform.

He had been attacked enough by Sam Decker. Now he was going to strike back, and he had an army willing to strike back at the former DEA agent turned private investigator. He would not allow Decker to continue to make a fool of him!

One of his men had taken over duties as cook after his servants had fled after Decker had attacked him home. The man was good at the job and the men in his private army were well fed before they formed up outside in the yard. Salvador had arranged for several airboats to be made available to his men from several different places in the 'glades.

Sam Decker and the boy were going to die, one way or another! Mateo Salvador swore it on the bodies of the men that Decker had already killed!

"Y'all pick some God awful times to get up," Jake Baca groused as he and Wally piled into an airboat. They had rented it in Fort Meyers and Wally had immediately headed them deep into the everglades.

"Well, Jake, you aren't exactly on vacation, now are you?" Wally asked.

"I suppose not. But I also didn't know I was expected to wake up before the crack of dawn."

"Dawn don't mind a bit. She likes her crack where it is," Wally grinned.

"Wally, that joke is older than I am," Jake groaned.

"But still good, Wally replied.

Hachi watched through binoculars as the two SUV's pulled up in front of Joe's airboat building. It was the same bunch from yesterday. They didn't look happy to find the closed sign on the door. One of the men took out a gun and shot into the door where the lock was. She winced at the sharp report. They pushed inside and came out a few minutes later. They had taken keys for three of the airboats, loaded their gear and roared away into the swamp. Hachi was glad that she had paid attention to the whisperings from the Great Spirit that had told her not to open this morning. She had a feeling that it had just saved her life.

Hachi pulled out her phone and dialed the number that Joe had given her. "Joe, those men came back, broke into the building and stole three of the airboats," Hachi said after her boss had answered.

"Are you okay?" Joe asked.

"Yes. The spirits warned me to stay away from work," she told him, knowing he would understand.

"You did well to heed them, Hachi. Go home, stay until you hear from me. If a week passes without word, the business is yours to do with what you will," Joe told her, hanging up. Hachi looked at the cell phone.

"I cannot sit this out, *Chilth-Keh*." Hachi began to paddle to the Quonset hunt. There were things she needed before taking to the swamp. Joe had already provided them.

"Well?" Sam Decker looked at Joe. He expected the worst, given Joe's expression.

"The hunters are coming. They broke into my store, stole three airboats. Hachi saw it."

"Is she okay?" Decker knew that his friend thought of the girl like his own daughter.

"She is. I told her to go home and wait a week."

"I heard that part, Joe. Do you think we won't survive this?"

"The spirits have not told me one way or another."

"Will she listen to you?"

"Probably not," Joe smiled.

"Welcome to parenthood," Sam grinned.

"Sam."

"Yes, Joe?"

"Shut up," Joe replied.

"Is everyone ready?" Salvador asked.

"All is prepared, Jefe," Red Jack told him. They had rented more than a dozen airboats to ferry the hunter-killer teams out into the everglades. That didn't include the three teams that were searching for the island of the Hidden Ones. Red Jack thought that perhaps it was overkill, but he didn't bother saying so to El Toro. That would be a folly that would get him killed.

Red Jack knew that the Cartel was growing tired of the expenses that El Toro was running up in his desire to eliminate Sam Decker. He had already been given certain orders regarding El Toro if things didn't go as El Toro planned.

They had been unhappy with the whole ordeal concerning the assassination of Kyle Mundy, and the assassination of Lacy Ryan. It had brought far too much heat down on them. The DEA and other agencies were cracking down on Flakka and its distributors.

While the drug was cheap to import and sell, the people making it were not ones to be trifled with. Not when they could bring the weight of an entire nation down on the people that were distributing it for them! The Cartel wanted to avoid that. The Chinese could cut them out if they wanted. There were enough Chinese gangsters in the United States for them to do that. The Triads were very active in the United States. The Cartel didn't want to give up a prime money maker. So if El Toro couldn't put an end to this war with Decker, he needed to be removed. One way or another. It would be better for the Cartel if they cleaned up their own mess, rather than the Chinese stepping it to do it.

"This is a problem," John Longfellow said as he watched El Toro's men board the airboats.

"Not as much as you might think," Rafael told him.

"Why is that?"

"Sam and Joe are out there. Wally and Jake are on their way to join them, as are we."

"So where does that leave us?"

"We are going to follow them and plug their escape route."

"How exactly do you plan to do that?" Longfellow asked.

"Because we are going to rent an airboat and follow them," Rafael replied with a grin.

"Of course we are. Why didn't I see that coming?"

"I have no idea."

Mark scuffed his feet as he headed for the dinning hall. He was ashamed of the way he had acted after his nightmare had awakened him during the night. He knew that Miss Julia was there for him, but he still didn't like being thought of as a crybaby that had nightmares.

Miss Julia was nice. Almost as nice as Miss Lacy had been. But he also knew that she wouldn't be around for ever. That wasn't her job. She was doing this to help Mr. Sam. That was pretty evident.

Mark had to wonder if she really cared about him? Miss Lacy had, that was evident. He wasn't so sure about Mr. Sam or Miss Julia. He knew that they liked him, but did they really care? It was a question that he couldn't answer.

"Mark, would you like to play?" a young girl asked. He had to think a minute to recall her name. It was Susie.

"Play what?" Mark asked.

"Tag. You are welcome to join our game," Susie told him.

"Okay," Mark grinned, glad for the invitation.

Julia watched as the young girl invited Mark to play. He had really brightened up when she had approached him. It was a good sign. Mark interacting with his peers was a good thing.

It meant that he was finally beginning to accept life here on the island. That would help him in the future. Mark didn't realize it, but it was a form of acceptance. That was something that he really needed.

Sam Decker finished off his breakfast and sat down on a log. They had slept in the stilt house, but that didn't make them safe. It had just gotten them thru the night. El Toro was going to come after them one way or another.

CHAPTER ELEVEN

The moon was climbing into the night sky and out away from the city, the velvet blackness was coated with bright white stars. Even over the roar of the airboat's engine, Decker felt at peace as the night air whipped past his face. The everglades at time seemed like an entirely different world, almost prehistoric in its beauty. The alligators were certainly a reminder of that, given that they were thought to be the last remaining descents of the dinosaurs.

They traveled for an hour before Joe shut off the engine and guided the boat up onto the small beach that surrounded the island where Decker and the others were constructing the stilt house. It was a long way from being done, but it would provide them with a place to sleep and a base of operations in the coming days.

Decker pulled out his tactical light and made sure that there were no slithery surprises between the boat and the stilt house as he and Joe carried their duffels full of weapons and supplies. Wally

111

would bring more when he and Jake came out tomorrow.

No snakes or spiders had made their way in during their absence. Same lit one of the hurricane lamps as Joe tossed up the bags. The sleeping bags were still in place, tightly rolled and sealed in plastic to keep out insect intruders. Decker cut the plastic and unrolled the two bags. He had slathered himself in insect repellent earlier and now lit some citronella candles to help keep the mosquitoes at bay. Finally, after they both had a cold beer, Decker and Joe crawled into the sleeping bags and went to sleep.

Mark Mundy tossed and turned in his sleep. The monsters had come back and were after him. He would run and hide but they kept finding him and he would escape and run some more.

It was hot and dark. Thick fog hung around him everywhere. He could hear them coming for him. He could hear the horrible thump of their footfalls as they chased him. He tripped over a tree branch and fell to the ground, his palms hit the mud and skidded forwards. Mark pushed to his feet. He could hear the loud explosions of gunshots, could hear the snap of bullets tearing through the air above his head. He could see the water. Mark jumped in, not caring what sort of horrors might be lurking beneath the calm surface!

Mark woke up, screaming. The sound snapped Julia awake and she moved instantly to the other bed and slipped her arms around Mark. "I'm here, Mark. I'm here," she whispered, doing everything in her power to comfort the boy. She could feel his tiny body shaking against her as he was wracked with sobs.

Miami, Florida.

Red Jack tried to sleep, but he couldn't. He was too wired up over the events of the day. El Toro was almost out of control now, totally enraged by the actions of Sam Decker and his friends.

They had in just a few days, crippled El Toro's criminal empire to the very brink of destruction. It continued to amaze Red Jack that they had done so without inflicting harm on a single innocent soul.

Finally, he could take it no more and threw the covers off of him. Red Jack stood and headed out of the bed room. In the living room, he poured himself three fingers of whiskey and added two ice cubes to it. He took a sip and reveled in the way it felt as it burned its way down to his stomach.

Right now, El Toro was far more dangerous to the cartels than his enemies were. He could have to contact Alvarez and see what he wanted to do with El Toro. Alvarez would have answers. Red Jack took another drink of the whiskey. The burn felt good as it spread through his body. The alcohol was relaxing him. Red Jack tossed back the rest of what was in the glass, setting it on the night stand. He lay back on the bed and pulled the covers up over him. He closed his eyes, and was soon sleeping soundly.

Morning.

Mateo Salvador opened his eyes. He felt invigorated. He showered and dressed, not in a suit as he normally would, but in camouflage fatigues and combat boots. They were actually hunting clothes, but they felt more like an army uniform.

He had been attacked enough by Sam Decker. Now he was going to strike back, and he had an army willing to strike back at the former DEA agent turned private investigator. He would not allow Decker to continue to make a fool of him!

One of his men had taken over duties as cook after his servants had fled after Decker had attacked him home. The man was good at the job and the men in his private army were well fed before they formed up outside in the yard. Salvador had arranged for several airboats to be made available to his men from several different places in the 'glades.

Sam Decker and the boy were going to die, one way or another! Mateo Salvador swore it on the bodies of the men that Decker had already killed!

"Y'all pick some God-awful times to get up," Jake Baca groused as he and Wally piled into an airboat. They had rented it in Fort Meyers and Wally had immediately headed them deep into the everglades.

"Well, Jake, you aren't exactly on vacation, now are you?" Wally asked.

"I suppose not. But I also didn't know I was expected to wake up before the crack of dawn."

"Dawn don't mind a bit. She likes her crack where it is," Wally grinned.

"Wally, that joke is older than I am," Jake groaned.

"But still good, Wally replied.

Hachi watched through binoculars as the two SUV's pulled up in front of Joe's airboat building. It was the same bunch from yesterday. They didn't look happy to find the closed sign on the door. One of the men took out a gun and shot into the door where the lock was. She winced at the sharp report. They pushed inside and came out a few minutes later. They had taken keys for three of the airboats, loaded their gear and roared away into the swamp. Hachi was glad that she had paid attention to the whisperings from the Great Spirit that had told her not to open this morning. She had a feeling that it had just saved her life.

Hachi pulled out her phone and dialed the number that Joe had given her. "Joe, those men came back, broke into the building and stole three of the airboats," Hachi said after her boss had answered.

"Are you okay?" Joe asked.

"Yes. The spirits warned me to stay away from work," she told him, knowing he would understand.

"You did well to heed them, Hachi. Go home, stay until you hear from me. If a week passes without word, the business is yours to do with what you will," Joe told her, hanging up. Hachi looked at the cell phone.

"I cannot sit this out, *Chilth-Keh*." Hachi began to paddle to the Quonset hunt. There were things she needed before taking to the swamp. Joe had already provided them.

"Well?" Sam Decker looked at Joe. He expected the worst, given Joe's expression.

"The hunters are coming. They broke into my store, stole three airboats. Hachi saw it."

"Is she okay?" Decker knew that his friend thought of the girl like his own daughter.

"She is. I told her to go home and wait a week."

"I heard that part, Joe. Do you think we won't survive this?"

"The spirits have not told me one way or another."

"Will she listen to you?"

"Probably not," Joe smiled.

"Welcome to parenthood," Sam grinned.

"Sam."

"Yes, Joe?"

"Shut up," Joe replied.

"Is everyone ready?" Salvador asked.

"All is prepared, Jefe," Red Jack told him. They had rented more than a dozen airboats to ferry the hunter-killer teams out into the everglades. That didn't include the three teams that were searching for the island of the Hidden Ones. Red Jack thought that perhaps it was overkill, but he didn't bother saying so to El Toro. That would be a folly that would get him killed.

Red Jack knew that the Cartel was growing tired of the expenses that El Toro was running up in his desire to eliminate Sam Decker. He had already been given certain orders regarding El Toro if things didn't go as El Toro planned.

They had been unhappy with the whole ordeal concerning the assassination of Kyle Mundy, and the assassination of Lacy Ryan. It had brought far too much heat down on them. The DEA and other agencies were cracking down on Flakka and its distributors.

While the drug was cheap to import, and sell, the people making it were not ones to be trifled with. Not when they could bring the weight of an entire nation down on the people that were distributing it for them! The Cartel wanted to avoid that. The Chinese could cut them out if they wanted. There were enough Chinese gangsters in the United States for them to do that. The Triads were very active in the United States. The Cartel didn't want to give up a prime money maker. So, if

El Toro couldn't put an end to this war with Decker, he needed to be removed. One way or another. It would be better for the Cartel if they cleaned up their own mess, rather than the Chinese stepping it to do it.

"This is a problem," John Longfellow said as he watched El Toro's men board the airboats.

"Not as much as you might think," Rafael told him.

"Why is that?"

"Sam and Joe are out there. Wally and Jake are on their way to join them, as are we."

"So where does that leave us?"

"We are going to follow them and plug their escape route."

"How exactly do you plan to do that?" Longfellow asked.

"Because we are going to rent an airboat and follow them," Rafael replied with a grin.

"Of course, we are. Why didn't I see that coming?"

"I have no idea."

Mark scuffed his feet as he headed for the dining hall. He was ashamed of the way he had acted after his nightmare had awakened him during the night. He knew that Miss Julia was there for him, but he still didn't like being thought of as a crybaby that had nightmares.

Miss Julia was nice. Almost as nice as Miss Lacy had been. But he also knew that she wouldn't be around forever. That wasn't her job. She was doing this to help Mr. Sam. That was pretty evident.

Mark had to wonder if she really cared about him? Miss Lacy had, that was evident. He wasn't so sure about Mr. Sam or Miss Julia. He knew that they liked him, but did they really care? It was a question that he couldn't answer.

"Mark, would you like to play?" a young girl asked. He had to think a minute to recall her name. It was Susie.

"Play what?" Mark asked.

"Tag. You are welcome to join our game," Susie told him.

"Okay," Mark grinned, glad for the invitation.

Julia watched as the young girl invited Mark to play. He had really brightened up when she had approached him. It was a good sign. Mark interacting with his peers was a good thing.

It meant that he was finally beginning to accept life here on the island. That would help him in the future. Mark didn't realize it, but it was a form of acceptance. That was something that he really needed.

Sam Decker finished off his breakfast and sat down on a log. They had slept in the stilt house, but that didn't make them safe. It had just gotten them thru the night. El Toro was going to come after them one way or another.

CHAPTER TWELVE

Scorpion Cay, Florida Keys.

"You did right to call me, Monica," Special Agent Myra Dish said as she settled into the chair across from her. She had an oval-shaped face, high cheekbones, full lips and a pert little nose that had just the hint of an upturn.

"I thought so," Chief Sinclair nodded. She had liked Myra Dish from the moment that they had met. Dish was a tough, no nonsense cop, just like she was.

"Did you really lock that guy in the boat with Decker's cat?"

"He was getting ready to break in anyway. I just gave him a taste of what he would have gotten if I hadn't caught him first. Plus, it was a bit of payback for him shooting Nora," Monica shrugged.

"One of these days, I want to meet that cat," Myra chuckled.

"I am sure I can arrange it," Monica smiled.

"How are things going between you and Mayor Duval?"

"About the same, except I no longer feel like I have a target on my back."

"Don't get too comfortable with that. I think that Lacy Ryan's murder brought too much heat and she just put her plot on hold."

"I suspect you may well be right about that. Myra, I need to get the good on Marie Duval and put her away."

"I've got a couple of good people working on that," Dish told her.

Marie Duval was seething with rage! El Toro and his hitman had blown everything by killing Lacy Ryan instead of Chief Sinclair. Now there was still too much heat to make any further action against the Chief of Police, especially with FDLE agents and DEA agents thicker than fleas on a dog's back.

She still hadn't heard back from the two guys from Miami that she had hired to blow Decker's boat up. They should have called an hour ago to let her know the job was done. Was she doomed to work with fools? She took a gulp of wine, finishing the glass, and then poured herself another.

Marie walked to the stereo and selected a CD full of New Orleans Jazz. The music started to play and it reminded her of home. Dancing and laughing in the French Quarter until the wee hours of the morning. Marie hummed along as she drank, slowly starting to sway to the music. She closed her eyes and let the music flow into her and take over her soul…

The Everglades.

The sky was pink as the sun began to climb into the sky. Joe had hidden the airboat very close by, where they could get to it easily in an emergency but where it could not be spotted by their hunters. Decker was wearing a tactical vest and camo BDU's over black combat boots with the Panama lugged soles. They were far superior for slogging through mud than the older Vietnam-era boots. He had an M-16 slung cross-body from left shoulder to right hip. An O.D. messenger bag filled with loaded magazines hung from his right shoulder to his left hip. His Browning Hi-Power 9mm hung under his left arm. There were extra magazines for it in the bag as well.

He had a camouflage do-rag over his red hair. Decker took time to paint his face with green, brown, and black streaks. He added it to his bare arms as well. Once he was sure that he would blend with his surroundings, he stepped out of the stilt house and climbed down the ladder. Joe was already outside. He had on a dark green tee shirt that was stretched to neat ripping point by his massive muscular chest and a pair of tight jeans, and knee high moccasins. He wore a knife sheathed on his belt and carried a handmade longbow and arrows that he had made himself. He also carried a .44 Magnum revolver holstered on his waist, with extra shells. The gun belt had been a gift from Wally.

"They are coming," Joe said.

"Let me guess, the spirits?" Decker snorted derisively.

"Don't underestimate them my friend."

"They have saved your life on many occasions."

"So, you keep telling me."

"Just because you do not believe, doesn't mean that they aren't real," Joe said.

"Right," Decker sighed. Then Joe simply vanished leaving Decker alone in the clearing. He hated when Joe pulled that particular stunt. It always unnerved him. One second he was there, the next he was gone. Decker shook his head and headed for the shoreline. He needed to find a good blind to watch for those who were hunting him.

"Are we there yet?" Jake Baca asked.

"Almost, Jake," Wally Norwood replied.

"Good. I'll be glad to get my feet on dry ground again."

"There ain't a lot of dry ground in the Everglades, Jake. But there is solid ground."

"That will work for me, Wally," Jake replied, shouting to be heard over the roar of the airboat's engine. The airboat slid across the giant marshland that was the Everglades, heading deeper into its heart.

"How far behind them do you think we are?" John Longfellow yelled.

"About fifteen to twenty minutes by my guess," Rafael yelled back as he guided the airboat along the channel.

"Good to know," John yelled back. He watched their surroundings and was shocked to see a huge alligator slide off one of the islands and into the water. It had to have been at least twenty feet long. John suppressed a shiver.

Hachi paddled along. She had seen snakes as big around as her thighs coiled in branches, hanging above the channels. For the moment, they were still sluggish in the cooler morning air. She would hate to be under one once the sun climbed higher into the sky and the reptiles grew livelier!

Instinctively, she headed for the Island of the Hidden Ones. She felt that she would be needed there more than anywhere else. There were many warriors there who could protect the island, but she had been told by the spirits that she would be needed there. She would not disappoint the spirit!

Mateo Salvador stood, perched on the prow of the airboat, an AK-47 clutched in his fists. The wind blew past his face, pushing his hair out behind him in the slipstream. Today, he would face Sam Decker and today he would kill him!

A deep-seated rage boiled down deep within him. It was bad enough that Decker had violated his home to threaten him. Then he had burnt down his stash houses, robbed his dealers, blown up his car and several out buildings, blown up his warehouse, and worst of all, had blown up his yacht!

Decker and his men moved like ghosts, in and out without being noticed. El Toro growled in frustration. Also, Marie Duval had blown him off, telling him that his money meant nothing anymore and that she was going to make sure his pipeline through the Keys would be shut down. Once he was done with Decker, he would return to Scorpion Cay and make that foolish bitch remember who was the boss!

Island of the Hidden Ones.

Julia Sinclair watched from the inside of the great hall which doubled as school during the day. Some of the tribal children had invited Mark to join them in their games and for the first time since she had met him, Mark was smiling and laughing and playing like a normal ten-year-old boy. It made her heart swell with joy.

She wondered how long it had been since Mark had laughed and played before this day. She was pretty sure that it had been a while. Julia glanced at her watch. Jessica Harmon should be arriving soon. One of the tribal elders had gone to Fort Meyers to meet her and bring her out.

Julia would feel better once Dr. Harmon had a chance to talk to Mark and evaluate him, maybe suggest some things that Julia could do to help him. She grabbed a bottle of water and opened it, taking a long pull. Soon, recess would be over and the kids would be coming back inside to start their afternoon classes.

Scorpion Cay, Florida Keys.

Kimberly Allen frowned at Josie McCoy's back. McCoy had been hired to replace Lacy Ryan as the City Attorney by Mayor Duval. Miss McCoy was nice enough, but she acted strange around Kimberly, as if she didn't trust her. That was fine, because Kimberly didn't trust her either.

"Kimberly, do you know where Miss Ryan kept her appointment planner?" McCoy asked.

"Her personal calendar she kept in her purse, so Mr. Decker probably has it now. Her business planner would be on her computer. I mean on your computer," Kimberly replied.

"Okay, thank you. I know this has to be awkward, me coming in like this and taking over. I've heard nothing but good things about my predecessor. It was awful, what happened to her," McCoy said.

"It does feel a little strange. Miss Ryan was my mentor. She hired me and she was teaching me the ins and outs of what this office does," Kimberly replied.

"It sounds like the two of you were pretty close," McCoy observed.

"We were. She was my boss, but she was also my friend. I could talk to her about anything."

"I hope we can build that same sort of relationship, Kimberly."

"I hope so too," Kimberly said. However, she had a feeling that would never happen. There was something off about Josie McCoy. Kimberly had felt it from the first time she had met her. She gave off the same vibe as Mayor Duval. That she couldn't be trusted.

It helped Kimberly make the decision that she had been thinking about since Lacy had been murdered. After she got off work, she was going to head over to the police station and put in her application with Chief Sinclair. One thing was for sure, she couldn't work much longer for Josie McCoy!

Special Agent Myra Dish sat in her car, keeping an eye on Mayor Duval's office. Why, she wondered, had the mayor hired the guys from Miami to blow up Sam Decker's boat? What did she stand to gain from that? It was a puzzle. Unless? Could it be that simple? She pulled out her cell phone and dialed headquarters in Tallahassee.

"Hey, Dish. How are things down in the Keys?" Whit Brandenburg asked. Whit was one of the best intelligence nerds in the FDLE. There was nothing that he couldn't find out if he set his mind to it.

"I need you to do some digging for me, Whit." Dish told him.

"Sure thing, Dish. What do you need?"

"I want everything you can find on Marie Duval, the Mayor of Scorpion Cay, and on a drug lord named Mateo Salvador, aka El Toro. I have a sneaking suspicion that they are connected, but I need proof."

"I'll get right on it and call you as soon as I know something," Whit replied.

"Thank you, my friend," Myra told him and broke the connection. If they were connected, as she suspected, that meant that Marie Duval was also involved in Lacy Ryan's murder.

The Everglades.

Red Jack wiped the sweat from his face. He hated the swamp. Hated it with a passion. He far preferred the dry heat of the Mexican desert. The airboats were searching in a grid pattern, each about a mile apart from the nearest companion boat. Five to six hardened killers per boat, plus the driver. More than sixty men were searching the swamp for Sam Decker and his companions.

The sun beat down on them from above, drawing the moisture out of their skin like water from a sponge. He opened a plastic bottle of warrior and drained it in just a few swallows.

He had been amazed by the things he had seen out here. He looked skyward and noticed several buzzards circling around in the blue sky above. They usually only circled where dead things were. Suddenly, the water beside the boat erupted in a violent splash!

Chapter Thirteen

The airboat lifted into the air and sent its passengers tumbling into the water. The airboat smashed upside down and exploded into flames. Red Jack fought his way to the surface even as the sound of the explosion echoed across the 'glades. He spotted an island and started swimming for it. Lingering in the dark waters of the 'glades could be very dangerous. Alligators, crocodiles, snakes, sharks, komodo dragons, all sorts of apex predators called these waters their home!

He hadn't seen what had caused the explosion, but he realized that he was damned lucky to be alive! The sound of the blast was still echoing across the water as he struck for the island. Three others were swimming as well. Two were just gone. Red Jack shivered as he searched the water around him with his eyes. Death could be lurking just beneath the surface!

Red Jack scrambled onto the small island along with the other survivors of the blast. He stood, searching the surroundings for evidence of what had caused the blast. Nothing. Shit!

"What the hell happened back there, Jefe?" one of the street soldiers asked.

"I don't know," Red Jack admitted. "I saw a small splash just ahead of us and then boom and we were all airborne."

"Somebody fired a grenade launcher at us. Probably high-explosive. If it had hit the boat, none of us would be alive now," Perez said.

"How do you know this?" Red Jack asked.

"I used to be in the army. I learned shit there."

"Good enough," Red Jack nodded.

"So, what do we do now?" Perez asked.

"We wait," Red Jack sighed.

Two miles away, one of the airboats was circling around a good-sized island. Finally, the driver aimed for a sandy beach and cut the throttle. The engine died and the boat's forward momentum drove it up onto the beach. The six men aboard piled off onto solid ground. They were run by one of El Toro's captains, a guy named Julio. Like Perez, Julio was ex-military. He had been a Marine.

He had hand-picked his crew. All of them were ex-soldiers.

They were a tight, well-trained, and well organized group. Julio made sure of that. He drilled his men twice a week in an abandoned warehouse where he had set up his own private "kill-house". A shooting range with surprise pop-up targets, only in this one, the 'bad guys' were cops. Julio and his crew were El Toro's top crew of enforcers.

Julio's second-in-command was a beefy guy named Santos. Julio waved him over. "What you want us to do, Julio?"

"I want you and your boys to sweep left, we'll sweep right, meet on the other side. I got a funny feeling about this island," Julio confided.

"I know what you mean. I felt like we were being watched while we were circling around it. You think it might be this Decker and some of his boys?"

"I don't know. But somebody was watching us. I want to know who it was."

"If they are here, we will find them," Santos said. Julio nodded and gathered his three men and headed along the shore to the right side of the island. Santos took his two and headed left.

Julio couldn't shake the feeling that he was being watched. So far, they hadn't spotted anyone. But the island and the surrounding area had grown deathly silent. Sweat was pouring down his face, the cloth tied around his skull was already soaked and beyond absorbing any more moisture. He wiped the sweat away from his eyes with the back of his left hand. *Madre Dios?* What was that awful smell? A slight breeze carried it on the wind. It smelled worse than a skunk, more pungent. One of his men let out a shrill scream and Julio spun towards him and looked into the face of a nightmare!

Jake Baca watched the small island that Red Jack and his men had taken refuge on after Wally and put a 40mm HE round in the water just as their boat drove over it. The round had detonated and flipped the big airboat, sending it tumbling over and over through the air before crashing down into the black waters of the Everglades. Two men had never surfaced, though Jake had thought he saw one body being dragged away by a big gator.

"So how comfortable are we going to let them get?" Jake asked.

"Oh, I think we have let them get about as comfortable as they are going to get. Are you ready to have some fun, Jake?" Wally asked.

"You know it, Compadre."

"Then let the good times roll," Wally said as he sent another 40mm grenade soaring towards the island. It hit a tree and exploded, showering the men with splinters and branches. Jake lifted his rifle to his shoulder, took aim and fired. One of the men dropped, a bloody hole in his chest. Wally dropped another round on top of them, but this one made it to ground level, sending a geyser of dirt into the air as shrapnel sliced into the few survivors. Jake fired again and the man known as Red Jack hit the dirt, the top of his head gone. Wally dropped in two more grenades and finished any survivors. He looked over at Jake. "That was fun. Now let's go find us some more!"

"You're the boss," Jake grinned back and they made their way to their small boat. Jake untied the lines and pushed it off the beach before jumping inside and taking a seat. Wally fired up the outboard motor and guided the small boat away from the island and back into the hunt.

Julio watched in terror as the big hairy thing tore his man's arm from his body and tossed the rest up into a tree. Julio lifted his M-16 to fire but the creature vanished as if it had never been there. The street soldier dropped to his knees, mutter prayers and crossing himself as he watched his man in the tree bleed out. What sort of monster was that? El Toro had described Decker as a Demon from Hell. Julio had thought that his boss had been exaggerating. Now he wasn't so sure!

"Everybody, get back to the boat! Now!" Julio screamed; turning and running back to the boat. One the other side of the island, Santos was faring no better. He and his men had also encountered another of the skunk apes. It had dropped down from them from above, long arms swinging massive fists, knocking two of the men down and sending one flying into the water. That man hit with a splash! The large hairy creature turned to Santos, baring sharp teeth and growling at him. Santos opened fire and the creature roared with pain as the bullets ripped into its flesh. Santos turned and ran, heading back towards the boat, leaving the dead men and the wounded creature behind him.

The man that had landed in the water splashed back to the surface, unaware that danger was behind him until massive jaws slammed shut on his sides. Ribs snapped under the pressure of those massive jaws, internal organs were crushed, blood sprayed out of his mouth. He was already dead when the massive gator dragged him under the water in a death roll.

Julio was cutting the lines and pushing the boat out into the water when Santos came running out of the woods. He jumped on the airboat as Julio scrambled over the side. Santos was in the driver's seat and fired the engine, the big blade roaring to life as he backed away from the island, one he was far enough away, he sent the ship shooting away in a long curve, heading back to where they had started the hunt from!

On the island, the larger of the skunk ape found the wounded one. A cry of anguish ripped from its monstrous throat. It cradled the young female to its breast. Tears leaked from its large eyes. Then it stood, beating its chest with massive fists and roaring out an angry cry.

"What the hell was that?" Sam Decker asked, hearing the angry cry echoing across the waters of the great swamp.

"That was one of the guardians. Those fools have angered the first people. They will all die in the swamp," Joe replied.

"You are telling me that sound was a skunk ape? Florida's original Bigfoot?" Decker looked at him, shocked.

"Just because you don't believe my friend, doesn't mean that they are not real," Joe replied.

"I'll be damned."

"Probably," Joe nodded.

"Joe…"

The Island of the Hidden Ones.

"Dr. Harmon, how nice to meet you," Julia said as she watched the older woman climb out of the canoe. Jessica Harmon was tall for a woman, with long legs and long brown hair tied back in a ponytail. She was wearing khaki cargo pants, hiking boots, and a khaki shirt with the sleeves rolled up a quarter length. She also had on a long-billed boater's cap. An Olive Drab Messenger bag hung from her left shoulder to her right hip. Her make-up was minimal, restricted to a pale pink lipstick.

"You are Miss Sinclair?" Dr. Harmon asked.

"I am. I'll take you to where Mark is."

"Lacy called me about him just a couple of days before her death and told me about his case," Jessica said.

"Well, Mark witnessed her death as well, at his father's funeral," Julia explained.

"That poor kid. How is Sam handling things?"

"I didn't realize you knew him," Julia looked surprised.

"We met through a mutual friend on Key West," Jessica smiled.

"Rick Marlow, my sister's friend," Julia nodded.

"Your sister?"

"Chief Monica Sinclair of the Scorpion Cay Police Department. She and Marlow worked together up in New York City," Julia explained.

"Interesting. So, where is Mark?" Jessica asked.

"Engaged in a game of tag, at the moment. Follow me please," Julia smiled and turned and walked off. Jessica Harmon followed her.

Mark Mundy hid behind the wide tree. He could see Samantha and Little Joe just a few feet away. They were searching for him, but so far, he had managed to remain hidden. Ted ran over and joined them. Mark smiled as he watched Ted wave his arms in the air. None of them had been able to find him.

"Ally Ollie oxen free!" Sam called. Mark stepped out of hiding.

"Here I am," he said, his voice making them jump.

"How did you do that?" Samantha asked, surprised.

"Seminole Joe taught me a few things," Mark shrugged.

"The Shaman is a good teacher," Samantha admitted. "How do you know him?"

"He is a friend of Mr. Sam, my guardian," Mark explained.

"Mark, could you come over here please?" Miss Julia called. Mark followed her voice. She was standing with another woman. Mark looked at his new friends.

"I have to go," he said.

"We'll find you later to play some more," Samantha smiled at him. It made Mark's heart beat just a little bit faster.

"Okay," he told her before running over to where Miss Julia and the other woman were waiting. "Hi Miss Julia," Mark said in greeting.

"Mark, this is Dr. Harmon. She is here to help you," Julia told him.

"Hi, Dr. Harmon," Mark said.

"Hello, Mark. Will you come with me so that we can talk for a bit?" Jessica asked him.

"Miss Julia?" Mark looked at her expectantly.

"It is okay, Mark. Miss Lacy made arrangements for this," Julia told him.

"Okay," Mark nodded, his expression grave. He took Jessica Harmon's hand and followed her back to Miss Julia's hut. The three of them went inside and Mark sat in one of the chairs that surrounded the small table that was the centerpiece of the room.

"Mark, I'm Jessica. I work with people that have been through a lot of trauma. Do you know what that means?" Jessica asked.

"It means people that have been hurt by things happening to the ones that they love," Mark replied softly.

"That's right, Mark. I k now you lost your mom, and then your dad, and then Miss Lacy. Do you think that applies to you?" Jessica asked.

"Yes, it does," Mark admitted.

"Okay, that is good. What I want you to do is to start telling me what it made you feel like when your mom died," Jessica explained.

Chapter Fourteen

"When Mommy and Daddy told me that Mommy was sick, it made me feel sad. But when she was gone, it made me feel really angry," Mark said, looking down at the scuffed toes of his sneakers.

"How did you deal with that anger, Mark?" Dr. Harmon asked, her tone was at once, both soothing and gentle.

"I got mad for no reason, and threw a lot of fits," Mark replied, his voice very soft, almost too soft to be heard.

"What did your Dad do when you acted out like that?"

"He would pick me up in a big hug and holkd me and tell me how much he loved me."

"How did that make you feel?"

"It made me feel bad, because how could Daddy still love me when I was acting so bad," Mark sighed his bottom lip quivering with emotion.

"Do you doubt that your Daddy loved you?" Dr. Harmon asked.

"No, I know that he did."

"What about when your Daddy got sick? When he started having the headaches?"

"It scared me. I was afraid he was going to leave me all alone."

"That is a pretty scary feeling, isn't it?" Mark nodded his head, refusing to look at her. His fingers were picking at a thread on his jeans.

"Mark, will you talk to me some more, later?" Jessica Harmon asked.

"I think I'd like that," Mark said, nodding his head.

"Go wash up, Mark. It's almost time for supper," Julia told him. Mark nodded and left the room.

"That boy is dealing with a lot of stuff," Jessica shook her head.

"Can you help him?" Julia asked.

"I can, but it is going to be a process. Do you think it will be okay if I stay here a few days? I can learn a lot about Mark from watching him as well as talking to him."

"I can arrange that," Julia told her.

"Thank you," Jessica smiled warmly at her.

Gordo Habanera ducked as a bullet hit the spinning propeller blade behind him, shatter the wooden prop which ripped through the mesh cage that enclosed it. The airboat glided across the water, all momentum bleeding off in the drag of the water.

"Anybody see where that came from?" Gordo called as he dropped from the driver's seat to the bottom of the airboat.

"N---," Hernando Martinez started to say as a bullet ripped through his open mouth and blasting out through his spine to sever his head from his body. The head tumbled to the deck as his body toppled over the side of the boat to splash into the water. Suddenly, everybody was hugging the deck as single shots tore the boat engine to pieces.

"Boys, I think we are fucked. There's no land above water nearby, which means we would have to swim for it," Gordo sighed.

"Fuck that. Get on the radio and call for help!" one of the men said. At that moment, a well-aimed shot hit the radio hanging from the driver's seat, shattering it into a million pieces!

"This is going to be a long day," Gordo sighed stoically.

Scorpion Cay, Florida Keys.

Monica Sinclair looked up when somebody walked into her office. She was surprised to see that it was Kimberly Allen, Lacy Ryan's former assistant. "Hello, Kimberly, what may I do for you?" Monica asked.

"Is there anything new about who killed my boss?" Kimberly asked.

"Sadly, no, Kimberly," Monica told her.

"I think the Mayor had something to do with it," Kimberly blurted.

"The Mayor? You've got my attention," Monica told her. "Why do you think so?"

"Lacy and the Mayor were arguing a couple of days before she was killed."

"What were they arguing about?"

"They were arguing about you."

"Me?" Monica asked, pretending surprise.

"Yes, you. And now, Josie, Lacy's replacement has been going through all of her files and asking a lot of questions about you,' Kimberly told her.

"What kind of questions?"

"About you and Mr. Decker, how close you have been, and how much Lacy might have confided in him."

"That is interesting news," Monica nodded.

"I was wondering, do you have any openings in the department? I like working for the City, but I don't want to work for Josie McCoy a minute longer than I have to. I don't trust her!" Kimberly said adamantly.

"You aren't alone in that, Kimberly. Let me get you an application," Monica smiled at the girl. She appreciated her sincerity.

"Thank you Chief. More than you can ever know," Kimberly told her.

The Everglades.

El Toro sat on the airboat waiting as his men swept yet another mangrove island. So far, they had found no sign of Decker and his people. But other members of his group had fallen out of contact. He had a bad feeling about that. Them falling out of touch made him nervous. Had they been attacked? Were they dead? At the moment, he had no way of knowing. He heard the sound of high-powered rifle fire echoing across the swamp.

He lifted his head, listening to the sound. It seemed to be coming from south of their position. He looked at the boat driver. "South, now!" he commanded, bracing himself for the rapid acceleration as the boat roared into a south turn and sped across the swamp.

The Island of the Hidden Ones.

"Tell me about the first time you met Miss Lacy," Jessica told Mark.

"She was really nice. I liked how she looked. Her hair looked almost like fire in the sun, but she liked me. I could tell from the minute we met," Mark said.

"How could you tell?"

"It was a feeling more than anything else. She picked me up and gave me a big hug. And she came after the bad men killed my daddy. She was nicer than Chief Monica. She made me feel good, even though I was sad," Mark explained.

"From what I hear, Miss Lacy was really good at that," Jessica nodded.

"Miss Lacy and Mr. Joe made me feel safe. I was a little nervous about meeting Mr. Sam, but he made me feel safe too," Mark told her.

"What did Miss Lacy and Mr. Sam tell you?"

"They told me that my Daddy had asked them to take care of me if anything happened to him," Mark explained.

"How did that make you feel, Mark?"

"I was scared at first. The Mr. Sam and Mr. Joe took me out into the swamp and we started building a house and listening to baseball games like I did with my Daddy."

"Did you like that?"

"I did, because when we were listening to the baseball games and building the stilt house, I didn't have to think about my daddy and what had happened to him.

"Don't you want to think about your Dad?" Jessica asked.

"Not yet, I don't. I don't like to think about seeing him shot and the blood spraying all over the place," Mark told her.

"I can understand that, Mark. You have to remember that your Daddy loved you, and he was doing his best to protect you," Jessica told him.

"I know that," Mark nodded. "But sometimes when I close my eyes, I still see him pushing me off of the pier and the bullets punching through him and filling the air with red mist. It was awful!" Mark shivered. Jessica leaned forward and hugged the boy, giving him reassurance that things were okay.

When he had calmed down again, Jessica sat back up. "Can you tell me about the day of your Daddy's funeral?"

"Do I have to?" he looked up at her with sad eyes.

"I think it might help if you do."

"Okay," Mark sighed.

Scorpion Cay, Florida Keys.

Marie Duval felt like a caged tiger, pacing in her office. If Mateo was going to ignore her calls and cut her off, well there were other places she could get help. Ones that might actually get the job done. She grabbed her keys and left the office. It was nearly five anyway. She should be able to reach Miami in a couple of hours.

She was pretty sure that she could get Dimitri to help her. And she knew that whoever he sent wouldn't fail. That was one thing that could be said about the Russians. When they took a job, they saw it through to the end. Now, at least she had a plan. One that would remove all the obstacles to her consolidating her power on the island, and even propel her into the statehouse!

Myra Dish was surprised to see Marie Duval charge out of her office and head for her car. Myra started her car and put it in gear, ready to follow the Mayor of Scorpion Cay. While she waited for Marie Duval to pull out from her parking space, Myra hit the call button on her phone for Chief Sinclair.

"What is it Myra?" Monica asked.

"You know any reason why Marie Duval would leave her office early and race off?" Myra asked.

"Nothing legitimate, that is for sure," Monica told her.

"Okay, well I am going to follow her and see where she goes. I'll let you know," Myra said as she hung up.

"That was interesting," Monica said.

"What?" Kimberly Allen asked. She was still filling out the application that Monica had given her.

"Myra is following Mayor Duval. She left her office in a hurry tonight," Monica replied thoughtfully.

"That does seem rather odd. The Mayor never leaves work early," Kimberly said. "Lacy told me that. She said ever since Mayor Duval took office, she was the first one in and the last to leave."

"Kimberly, filling out those forms is just a formality. You have a job. I'm starting you out as a dispatcher. When can you start?" Monica asked.

"First thing in the morning," Kimberly's face lit up.

"Okay. Come in at 8 a.m. and I'll have Dale train you on the radio. You'll be with him for a week and after that, I'm putting you on the afternoon shift from four to midnight. Dale has days and Rufus handles the night shift," Monica explained.

"Thank you so much," Kimberly told her.

"Oh, and don't bother giving notice to Ms. McCoy. I want to deliver that bit of news myself," Monica smiled.

The Everglades.

The sun was slowly starting to sink in the west. Mateo was concerned. He had lost communications with at least three of his crews. How had that happened? The mosquitoes were getting worse as the sun started to set, and an eerie silence had settled over the swamp.

It unnerved him. He had an unnerving feeling that somehow, he had gone from being the hunter to being the prey. He looked at Alejandro. "Call it a night. Tell everyone to head back to Miami. I don't think I want to spend a night out here," Mateo Salvador commanded.

"Sure thing, Boss. I don't want to spend the night out here either," Alejandro replied. He sent out the call. Only two teams acknowledged it out of the five that had come out that morning. Mateo had a bad feeling that maybe this time, he might well have gone too far!

Chapter Fifteen

It was getting dark quickly. A storm front had blown up out of the Gulf, bringing with it some high winds and ominous rumbles of thunder. The thick cloud cover was making it increasingly more difficult to find their way out of the swamp. A strange, almost unnerving silence had settled over the glades as the wind began to whistle through the mangroves and banyan trees. Spanish moss fluttered like living creatures undulating from tree branches like living things. Strange, undulating cries began to ring out from different points around this, raising goosebumps on El Toro's men's flesh and sending shivers racing down their spines.

"Boss, we need to find land. The storm is coming in fast. There is no way we will be able to make it back before it hit," Jesus Ibanez said.

"Shit! Okay, find an island. It looks like we are stuck out here for the night," Mateo Salvador ordered. Jesus nodded, using a spotlight mounted on the driver's chair. Thunder rumbled overhead and chain-lightning flashed in the dark clouds above. The boat was hitting waves that were making the ride pretty rough, and more than a few of this gang of hardened criminals were busy puking over the sides because of it. Finally, Jesus spotted a likely spit of land and sent the airboat running up onto the beach. The men quickly rolled off and made lines fast to several stout-looking trees. Then they made their way to higher ground where the trees afforded them at least a small measure of protection from the storm.

Other members of El Toro's kill teams were also forced to find shelter from the storm. Decker's people rallied at the stilt house, so they at least were able to stay dry and for the most part warm. They were also able to enjoy a warm meal and coffee, something El Toro's men could only wish for.

The strange cries sounded all across the swamp. And in the darkness, shadows began to move with a deadly purpose. Rain began falling in almost sold sheets, making it impossible to see.

The Island of the Hidden Ones.

The storm rolled in while Mark was talking to Dr. Harmon. He had already described the service for his father. He had just got to the part where they were starting back to their cars, his Daddy's American flag clutched to his chest.

"I heard a loud boom, like a gun shot, and then Mr. Sam was pushing me toward the car. He had a gun in his hand and was shooting behind him just like the police officers and Mr. Rafael and Mr. Joe. I heard somebody yelling awful things, and then Miss Lacy threw herself on me and rode me to the ground. In what seemed like forever, the shooting stopped. Miss Lacy didn't move, and I was starting to be even more scared because her body was pushing down one me and it was getting hard to breathe," Mark said.

"You were really frightened, weren't you?" Jessica asked.

"Yes. Finally, I managed to wiggle out from under Miss Lacy. That's when I saw the blood." Mark swallowed hard. "Mr. Sam got there then, and he was on his knees, holding her in his arms. Blood bubbles were breaking on her lips and running down her chin. She looked up at Mr. Sam and told him that she loved him, and then she looked at me and said she loved me too, and then she quit breathing. Mr. Sam, he just started to scream, looking up at the sky with Miss Lacy in his arms. Finally, Mr. Wally came and got me and took me to the car. An Ambulance came, but it was too late to help Miss Lacy. Mr. Joe and Mr. Wally brought me here and told me that as soon as it was safe, Mr. Sam would come and take me home," Mark said, starting to cry. His tears flowed freely and his whole body shook with the energy of his grief.

Jessica sat back, trying to make sense of it all as Julia gathered Mark in her arms and comforted him. That poor kid! He had watched three of the people that he had been closest to die, and the one that he had left had sent him off to a strange place until he could make sure that things were safe for the boy to return home. It was a stunning tale, and she wished she could talk to Sam Decker. Because while he had done the safest thing for Mark, it might well not have been the right thing.

Mark needed a solid presence in his life now more than ever. She didn't know Sam Decker well, but from what she had heard about him, she wasn't even sure that he was the best choice to raise this poor child. It was something that she would have to give a lot of thought to!

One thing was certain. Mark was going to need some intensive therapy, and he would need it for a while if he were ever to have a chance to put this behind him!

Miami, Florida.

Marie Duval pulled into the parking lot of Mango's Tropical Café. She knew that she would find Dimitri there. She might have to wait a bit, but she knew that he would come in. He liked to check on his properties personally. She parked her car, paid the cover charge and went inside. Marie took a seat at the bar and ordered a Cosmopolitan. The bartender was a heavily muscled guy named Sven. He had Nordic good looks and wavy blonde hair.

"Sven, when is Dimitri due?" Marie asked.

"He comes and goes on his schedule. He doesn't bother to tell his bartenders," Sven replied.

"Well, if this particular bartender wants to keep his job, he had better goddamn well call him and tell him I'm waiting on him," Marie smiled wickedly. Sven looked into her eyes for a moment and then headed for the phone that hung behind the bar. He dialed a number from memory and spoke quietly for a couple of minutes before hanging up and walking back.

"The boss will here shortly," he told her before turning and walking away. That was a show of defiance on his part. Marie knew that he would return to take her drink order. He was in deep enough shit after being rude to her and having to call Dimitri. He wouldn't want for Dimitri to arrive and find her without a drink in front of her.

Myra Dish sat outside Mango's Tropical Café. It didn't take long for her to make the beefy Russian security team that routinely patrolled the perimeter and swept the parking lot. That was why she had parked in a lot across the street. She called headquarters and got a quick rundown on the bar and the owner.

Mango's was currently showing Dimitri Renko as the owner. According to the Organized Crime Bureau, Renko was a lieutenant under Vasily Drushnekov, a ranking member in the Miami branch of the Russian Mafia. Myra pursed her lips in a silent whistle. The Russians were pretty fucking dangerous people to mess with. If Marie Duval was ready to climb into bed with them, things had just gotten even more serious for Monica Sinclair!

Thunder rumbled in the distance and rain drops began to splatter on her windshield as she dialed Monica Sinclair's cell number. The Police Chief of Scorpion needed to know about this sooner rather than later.

The Everglades.

"What are you thinking about, Sammy?" Wally asked as he squatted down next to Decker. Decker was looking out into the storm.

"Are we doing the right thing, Wally?" Sam looked at the man that had raised him.

"What does your heart tell you, Sammy?'

"I'm barely sure I have one left, Wally. I'm pretty sure mine was cut out when Lacy was shot down in front of me."

"What about Mark? Are you going to just leave him too?"

"I don't know what to do about Mark, Wally. I've never been a parent before."

"Nobody ever is until they find themselves with a kid, Sammy. I had never been a parent until I took you in, part of your Dad's dying wish. Kyle Mundy placed that same sort of trust in you. The question is, are you going to do what he asked or are you going to betray that trust?"

"That's a part of what I'm trying to figure out. Part of me wants to just end it all, go out in a blaze of glory avenging Lacy and Kyle, hoping that I die in the attempt," Decker sighed.

"What about the other part?" Wally asked.

"That part wants to honor both Lacy and Kyle by raising Mark. He's a good kid, Wally. But he's seen too much in too short of time. I don't know how to help him through that."

"Didn't Lacy set something up for him? To see a shrink of some kind?" Wally asked.

"Yes. Julia followed through and Joe had somebody meet her to take her to meet Mark. I haven't talked to Julia today though," Decker admitted.

"Maybe you should give Julia a call in the morning and see how things went. Maybe talk to Mark to so that he knows you haven't forgotten about him. He needs that reassurance. You did as well if I recall."

"I know I did, Wally. Have I ever thanked you for what you did for me back then?" Decker looked at the man that had finished raising him after his father died.

"You thank me every day, Sammy. You thank me by being a good man and by chasing bad guys and putting them away," Wally told him, reaching over to pat him on the shoulder.

"Well this time old friend, I'm saying the words. Thank you, Wally for making me a better person," Decker told him.

"You're welcome, Son. Now get some rest. We've got some bad guys to round up tomorrow," Wally said, standing. Wally walked over to his bedroll, pulled off his boots and crawled into his sleeping bag.

Sam Decker sat there looking out into the storm for a while longer. Finally, he stood and stretched good, and then headed for his own bedroll. Wally was right. Tomorrow, they had bad guys to catch. Not to kill. Sam Decker closed his eyes and was soon fast asleep.

Scorpion Cay, Florida Keys.

"Something is bothering you," Juan Santiago said as he looked at his wife. They were sitting up late, watching Casablanca on one of the stations from Miami. Juan loved the movie, being a romantic at heart. The children were all sleeping soundly.

"I'm worried about Sam and Rafael," Nora admitted.

"They can take care of themselves, Dear. You know that."

"I know they can. They've proved that time and again. But Sam has never been hurting like this. I'm afraid that he will do something stupid."

"Sam has many good friends with him. They will keep him grounded. Trust your brother and the rest of Sam's friends to keep him focused on doing what is right," Juan told her.

"How did you get so wise?" Nora asked her husband.

"I married a smart woman," he replied, kissing her.

"You're sure about this?" Monica asked Myra Dish.

"I'm sitting outside Dimitri Renko's club as we speak. Marie appears to be waiting for the owner to arrive," Myra told her.

"The Russians can be a real pain in the ass," Monica sighed.

"That is why I called to give you a head's up. I'm going to stick with Marie and see where she goes."

"Okay. Keep in touch," Monica told her before hanging up. Monica was sitting in her home. She looked at Bailey who had come bounding into the room when her phone rang. The big dog nudged her leg with her head. Monica reached down and scratched the dog behind the ears.

The dog butted her leg with her head once again and added a soft whine. "Okay, I'll let you out. But this is it for the night," she told the beagle/rottweiler cross. Monica stood and walked to the back door, opening it and letting Bailey out into the back yard. It would take the dog about ten minutes to do her business. Monica checked the doors to make sure all but the back one were locked. Finally, she returned to the back door and let Bailey in. She locked the back door and then headed for her bedroom. She needed to get some sleep.

Miami, Florida.

Marie looked up as Dimitri entered the restaurant. He was a striking man in his mid-to-late thirties. Thick brown hair parted on the left and slicked back with pomade. He had classic good looks and a muscular build that spoke of time spent on daily gym visits. He had blue eyes and a Van Dyke goatee. His suit was Armani, his shoes Gucci. Four men trailed behind him and she easily recognized them as bodyguards. He wasted no time and walked directly to her, taking the stool beside her.

"Marie, it has been a while," he greeted her.

Chapter Sixteen

It was growing late when Marie Duval left the Mango Tropical Café. Myra Dish had slipped out and planted a GPS tracker on the Mayor of Scorpion Cay's car. It would give her up to the minute access to the Mayor's whereabouts, at least her car's whereabouts at any given time. It would also keep track of where and when the Mayor went.

She was pretty sure the Mayor would be heading back home in time to catch the last ferry to the island from Duck Key. She watched as Mayor Duval climbed back into her car and pulled out onto the street. Dish was just a few seconds behind her. The fury of the storm was intensifying and she had her windshield wipers working at top speed and it was still hard to see. Lightning flashed across the sky, nearly destroying her night vision. The Mayor was no longer in front of her. Dish pulled to the curb and cursed before remembering she could track her on her cell phone. The Mayor had gone to a nearby hotel. Apparently, she was planning to spend the night in Miami.

That worked for Dish she was tired and could use a good night's sleep herself. She hated to admit it, but she was hungry and tired. She swung into hotel. She would call an order a pizza and a six-pack once she was in her room.

The Everglades.

Thunder and lightning ripped through the night, some of it was shaking the ground. Rain fell in almost solid sheets, making the refugee hit squads even more miserable. The mosquitoes showed no mercy even in the rain. One group of about twelve men had taken shelter on one of the larger islands that they had been able to find before the storm broke in its full fury.

They had managed to erect a small shelter and get a small fire going. It was burning hot enough to dry the wet wood they were forced to feed it because of the storm. But at least it helped drive the chill out of their bones. Shadows danced around them. Between the fire and the flashes of lightning, it added an eerie atmosphere. Those strange cries they had heard earlier already had them spooked.

So, when the first man sitting near the back vanished, it took them a few minutes to notice. Then a second man was jerked out of the light and into the darkness. They heard his scream and then their weapons came up and they all put the fire at their backs.

"What the hell is out there?" Simon Gustavo demanded.

"I wish I knew," Alberto Ribera whispered in reply.

"This goddam swamp is haunted," Luis Delgado said, his voice shaking with terror.

"Over there!" Pablo Sanchez screamed, firing his rifle into the shadows and burning out the magazine of his AK-47. Suddenly the tarp they had tied over the fire ripped loose and fluttered away on the wind. In seconds the fire was washed out by the rain, and they were all plunged into darkness. More men began to scream and as guns were fired, the muzzle flashes lit the darkness as things descended on them and soon the clearing was bathed in blood.

The Island of the Hidden Ones.

Jessica Harmon shivered as the thunder crashed outside. The storm had caused her to have nightmares. What not many people knew was that Jessica herself suffered from PTSD. She had a client commit suicide, and then she and another client had been stalked by a madman determined to kill them both. If not for the intersession of Rick Marlow, he might have gotten away with it.

Rick Marlow trusted Sam Decker. So did Monica Sinclair. It was obvious that Julia did too. Jessica wanted to talk to Decker. If that didn't happen, she would be forced to make a call to Child Services about Mark Mundy, and that was something she really didn't want to do. Mark was damaged enough already, without being put through the meat-grinder of family services. She needed to prevent that at all costs if the boy was to have any chance at all. Jessica took a drink of water from the bottle on the table beside her and closed her eyes. Soon she was once more, fast asleep.

Dawn.

The storm had ended sometime during the night. Decker was the first to awaken and he had climbed down and got a fire going in the fire pit so that they could cook breakfast. He filled a coffee pot with water, a filter, and sat it on a stone on the edge of the roaring fire. It would perk well enough.

"Good Morning," Wally told him as he climbed down the ladder. The old man looked fresh as a newborn baby.

"Good Morning," Decker replied.

"I'll start breakfast cooking, if you want to wake the others," Wally told him. Decker was more than happy to let Wally do the cooking. He climbed back up the ladder and woke the others up. Slowly they emerged from the stilt house and then headed into the brush to take care of business.

"So, what do we do now, Wally?" Decker asked.

"We have breakfast and then we go hunting," Wally replied.

"How many do you think survived the storm?" Decker asked.

"Not many," Joe said as he appeared out of nowhere, causing Decker to jump.

"Dammit Joe, I wish you would stop doing that," Decker growled at his friend.

"The guardians were hunting last night. They didn't get them all, but they did whittle down the numbers," Joe shrugged.

"You seem sure of that," Decker noted.

"I am," Joe shrugged. He poured himself a cup of thick black coffee.

Decker shook his head. While he liked and respected Joe, he was never quite sure that he believed all of the mystical talk that Joe spouted. Shaman or not, Decker believed in what he could see and touch.

After they had breakfast, Sam walked away from the others and pulled out a satellite phone. Julia had one just like it on the island of the Hidden Ones. Sam keyed in her number and waited for her to answer.

"Sam?" Julia sounded surprised.

"I wanted to see how Mark was doing," Decker told her truthfully.

"He seems to be making friends with the other kids. I'd call that a good sign," Julia replied.

"I would too," Decker told her. "Is he around? I'd like to talk to him.

"Give me a minute," Julia told him. She walked to Mark's room. He was just waking up.

"Mark, it is Mr. Sam. He wants to talk to you."
She handed Mark the sat phone.

"Hello?" Mark asked.

"How are you, Mark?" Decker asked.

"I'm okay. Doctor Harmon is helping me,"
Mark told him.

"I'm glad Mark. I'm getting close to
catching the man that murdered your Daddy, Mark.
Once I do that, I'll be coming to get you so we can
go home," Decker told him.

"To the boat or to the house?"

"To the house," Decker promised.

"Can we still go out on the boat?"

"Of course, we can, Mark. I want you to
promise me that you'll be good for Julia and Dr.
Harmon. This will be over soon and then we can go
home."

"I can do that Mr. Sam!" Mark replied, a
hint of joy in his voice.

"Can you give the phone back to Julia?"
Decker asked. A moment later Julia was back on
the line.

"I don't know what you said, but you clearly
made his day. Mark acts like he's walking on air,"
Julia told him.

"I told him that this is almost over and that
he and I will be going home soon," Decker replied.

"Well, I think he needed to hear that, and to
hear it from you. How much longer do you think it
will take?"

"A day, maybe two. No longer than that," Decker assured her.

"Good," Julia said and hung up.

"Did you talk to Mark?" Wally asked as Decker returned to the Stilt house.

"I did. I think we need to take the offensive and go after these assholes. I want to end this and bring El Toro to justice," Decker said quietly.

El Toro and his men huddled miserably as the sun began to climb into the sky. They had spent a cold, miserable, and frightening night huddling on the small island, getting pounded by cold rain and high winds. They were all soaked to the skin and shivering even though the temperature was quickly climbing with the sun. A couple of the boys were shivering bad, already in the throes of hypothermia.

El Toro was fueled by rage. His anger kept him warm against the wet clothing that lay against his skin. As the sun continued to rise, steam began to rise from their clothing as the bright rays began drying it. Sam Decker was going to pay for this. Perhaps even the entire island where he made his home would pay as well!

Miami, Florida.

Marie Duval finished her breakfast and prepared to check out of her hotel room. She felt rested and alert, ready to face the new day. She was pleased with the deal that she had worked out with Dimitri Renko. He had assured her that he would

166

send someone to Scorpion Cay to deal with Monica Sinclair within the next few days. Marie was glad of it, because she didn't trust Monica Sinclair to not come after her. She was aware that the police Chief had been growing more suspicious about her agenda for the small island. Lacy had been too. Her death had been a fortuitous accident, but one that had worked in Marie's favor.

Lacy's replacement was much more willing to follow the Mayor's lead. Josie McCoy was a lawyer she had hand-picked as soon as she had realized that Lacy was not going to co-operate with her agenda. Marie headed for her car. It was time to get back to the island.

FDLE Special Agent Myra Dish pulled out behind Marie Duval's car. The hit the causeway and headed south towards Highway One. This early, traffic was light, but it would still take them a couple of hours. Myra pulled out her cell phone and dialed Monica's number.

"Where are you, Myra?" Monica asked.

"Still in Miami, the Mayor decided to spend the night and drive home this morning. I decided to do the same," Myra replied.

"Probably a wise decision. Were you able to find anything out?"

"She hired the Russians to kill you."

"That could be a problem," Monica said, speculatively.

"It could. I want you to let me bring in more agents to watch your back," Myra told her.

"I don't need a bunch of new faces to keep track of, Myra."

"They won't be new faces, Monica. These will be hand-picked agents that I personally know and can vouch for," Myra said.

"I will hold you to that," Monica told her.

"I won't let you down," Myra sighed. She ended the call. She hoped that her boss would go along with what she had just promised. It was the only way to keep Monica safe from whatever Mayor Duval had planned.

The Island of the Hidden Ones.

Mark awakened early. He slipped out of the house and went to the communal restrooms to take care of business. He liked the dawn. The day was fresh and new. The sun was climbing into the sky, a bright burning orb that spread its life-giving glow across the land. Mark looked too the island nearby and saw one of the guardians for just an instant before it disappeared into the undergrowth.

A Skunk Ape! He had seen one of them. Mark dropped to his knees. The Florida Version of Bigfoot was supposed to be a myth, a legend of the swamp. But he had seen one with his own eyes!

Mark shook his head. Joe had told him about the guardians, but Mark had not really believed him. But now he had seen one with his own eyes. Shaking his head, Mark walked back to the house that he shared with Miss Julia and Miss Jessica. For the first time since he had come to the island, he felt safe.

Mark walked in just as Miss Julia looked around for him. "Mr. Sam is on the phone and he wants to talk to you," Miss Julia said with a smile.

Chapter Seventeen

Sam Decker carried his rifle to the boat. The others were loading up their gear as well. It was time to end this thing with El Toro. It was time to end it today, once and for all. If possible, he wanted to capture the man and make him stand trial. But failing that, he would put a bullet between the man's eyes. Either way, it wouldn't matter. Sam wanted this over and he wanted to get Mark back and settled into a routine. He and the boy needed to spend more time together getting to know each other. They were going to be together for the next decade if not more.

Decker was changing. It had started with Lacy and had grown during their relationship. Meeting Mark had changed him even more. He smiled to himself. Maybe he was finally growing up. He would give it some thought, maybe spend time with Dr. Harmon, or another therapist. Maybe it was time to make changes that would be good for him and Mark both.

Hachi had spotted one of the places where El Toro's men had taken shelter through the night. She had heard the calls of the ancient ones as they had moved about during the storm, but she did fear them because she was one of The People. The guardians and the Seminole had long lived in peace with each other.

She felt no fear of the Skunk Apes. She considered them part of the tribe. She smiled as they drifted away in the dawn, vanishing into the mists that hung over the early morning water, returning to their homes. Hachi paddled to a small island and dragged her canoe out of the water and into the brush to conceal it. She removed her crossbow and arrows. She would fight this battle too, but in the ways of her people.

Scorpion Cay, Florida Keys.

Kimberly Allen arrived at the Police Station early. She was ready to start her first day as a police officer, even if it was just as a dispatcher. Monica had given her three uniforms the night before. Kimberly had braided her hair and pinned it up in a bun on the back of her head. She looked very sharp in her uniform.

"Good Morning," Monica told her, greeting her at the dispatch counter with a fresh cup of coffee which Kimberly gladly accepted.

"Are you going to talk to Miss McCoy?" Kimberly asked, feeling a little nervous about not giving notice on her other City job.

"I'm going over there just as soon as I get you settled," Monica reassured her. She walked her into the radio room where Rufus Drake was surrendering his seat to Dale Kerwin. "Boys, this is Kimberly Allen, our new dispatcher. Dale, you train her for the next three days and then she'll be taking the 4p.m. to midnight shift."

"A pleasure to meet you," Rufus said, swallowing hard. His eyes almost seemed to be glazing over.

"Nice to meet you Kimberly. Have a seat and I'll show you how this mess works," Dale Kerwin smiled. Kerwin was a tall, handsome man with thick brown hair, brown eyes, and kind eyes. He had about a decade on Kimberly, but she thought he was a handsome guy.

"I look forward to it," Kimberly replied, taking a seat next to him. Rufus Drake hung his head. He was pretty sure that with Dale in the picture he stood no chance with the pretty new dispatcher. Monica caught his reaction and followed him out into the hallway.

"Rufus, I need to speak to you," Monica said, the tone of her voice making it an order. Rufus stopped and waited for her to reach him.

"What, Ma'am?" he asked.

"Rufus, Kimberly is barely 21 years old. I don't want you or Dale trying to take advantage of her. I've already talked to Dale about it. She is like family to me. Do you understand?" Monica asked. Rufus nodded.

"I understand," he said.

"I'm glad to hear it Rufus. I really am. Kimberly worked for Lacy over at the City's Attorney's office. She is one of my family," Monica explained.

"She's a pretty girl, Chief. I won't let nobody hurt her," Rufus explained.

"I'm counting on that Rufus," Monica told him before walking away. She wanted to talk to Josie McCoy and she wanted to do it before the interim City Attorney was ready for her. Monica climbed into her car and started the engine. A moment later she pulled out onto the street and headed for the City building.

Miami, Florida.

Dimitri Renko had finished his breakfast and was reading the Herald to see what was new in the city. The door to his study opened and Ivan Korsakov walked in.

"You sent for me?" Korsakov asked.

"I did, Ivan," Renko told him.

"How may I be of help?" Korsakov asked.

"I have a job for you."

"What is job?"

"I want you to kill the police Chief on an island called Scorpion Cay."

"I can do that."

"I hope so," Renko told him.

"This is very important," Dimitri said.

"It always is," Renko nodded.

The Everglades.

Nico Morales frowned as he looked at the rising sun. He wasn't sure where he and the men in his command were hiding. He hated the fact that they were hiding at all from a bunch of men that had once been cops. He turned and looked at his men. "Who besides me is ready to find that bastard Decker and end this shit?" he asked.

"We all are," Pablo Cruz announced as he readied his rifle for battle.

"Then let's do it! Let's get this bastard and take his head to El Toro!" Morales commanded. He and his men headed towards where they had left their boat the night before. Just then a huge python dropped down out of the branches above, sinking fangs into one of the men's neck as it coiled his body around it and began to squeeze. One of his companions shot the man between the eyes, knowing that the man was already dead.

The group started moving faster, keeping an eye on the trees as they did so. Finally, they reached the beach. There they found another problem. Several alligators were on the beach between them and where the boat was tied to two large mangroves.

"What the fuck!" Nico screamed in frustration. The only clear way to approach the boat would send them back into the trees. They would come out on the other side of the boat, away from the gators, but there could be a lot larger snakes hiding in the tree branches that would spread above their heads. They were, literally, between a rock and a hard place!

The group was bunched together, and the line of gators slowly began to advance. "We should be able to out run them," Nico said confidently.

"Those monsters are pretty damn fast, boss," Cruz whispered. Talking out loud didn't feel right. As if by using a loud voice might make the ancient reptiles attack them.

"Shoot them," Nico commanded. He and his men fired, and the creatures attacked!

El Toro and his crew were back on the water. They had spent a miserable night in the swamp, and the new day would be even more miserable. However, El Toro had no choice. Sam Decker had to die!

The sun had warmed them and dried their clothes as it climbed higher into the sky. The wind whipped his long hair behind him as the airboat speed across the swamp grass and water that made up one of the largest remaining ancient ecosystems in the United States.

Sam Decker stood slightly ahead of where Joe sat in the driver's seat of the airboat. He had one hand on the pistol-grip of his assault rifle, the other on his knee to help steady himself as the boat skimmed across the saw grass and water. Rafael stood to his left, his eyes also scanning for the enemy. Nearby, Wally was driving another airboat with John Longfellow and Jake Baca. They were in full hunting mode now.

This battle was going to end this day, one way or the other. It was down to the nut-cutting, root hog or die time. Either they would leave the swamp or El Toro would. But not both!

Scorpion Cay, Florida Keys.
"Monica, I'm back on the island," Myra Dish said as she rolled off the ferry, following Marie Duval.

"I'm glad to hear it, Myra," Monica Sinclair said, meaning it. She felt that she had met a kindred spirit in the FDLE Special agent.

"My people will be arriving on the next ferry and I'll make sure you meet them so you know who they are. Marie Duval is going to go down for what she has done!" Myra Dish said with conviction.

Marie Duval stopped at her house to shower and change clothes before heading into work at the Mayor's office. She was in a pleasant mood, knowing that Dimitri Renko would be sending someone to eliminate Monica Sinclair within the next twenty-four hours.

The Chief of Police was rapidly becoming a thorn in her side and she was more than ready to pull that thorn out and toss it into the trash. She would handle Decker herself when the time came.

He would be easy, compared to Monica. No man could resist her when she put her mind to it!

Josie McCoy was surprised when she got to the office and Kimberly Allen was not already there. She would have to file a disciplinary report on her. Eliminating Kimberly from her office was part of the reorganization that she and Mayor Duval had discussed. The Mayor wanted no remnants of Lacy Ryan in City Hall. Kimberly was certainly one of those.

Josie put on water for coffee and booted up her computer to check her appointments for the day. She was actually very surprised when Chief Sinclair walked into her office with a smile on her face. "Good morning, Chief. What may I do for you today?" Josie asked.

"I just wanted to let you know that Kimberly Allen won't be in today, or any day going forward," Monica told her.

"Why is that?" Josie asked, uncertain about what was going on.

"She no longer works for you," Monica said.

"What?"

"She no longer works for you," Monica told her drawing the words out, like she would for a person of limited intelligence.

"I don't understand," Josie shook her head.

"I hired her last night. She's my new dispatcher," Monica smiled sweetly.

"What?" McCoy asked, in shock over the announcement.

"I hired her as a dispatcher last night. It seems that she no longer wanted to work for this office, so I Okayed a lateral transfer to my department. I'm sure that I can count on you to let the Mayor know," Monica told her.

"Do you have the authority to do that?"

"I do. Tell Marie to come talk to me if she has a problem with it."

"I certainly will," Josie McCoy replied coolly. Monica smiled as she turned and walked out of the room.

Myra Dish watched from a distance as Marie Duval entered the building that housed her office. She powered down her windows, pretty sure she would be in for a long wait before the Mayor went anywhere else this morning.

The Island of the Hidden Ones.

"Miss Julia," Mark whispered. Julia looked over at her young charge.

"Yes, Mark?" she asked, curious about what he wanted.

"I saw something this morning on my way to talk to Mr. Sam on the telephone," Mark told her.

"What did you see, Mark?" Julia asked curiously.

"I saw a Skunk Ape. He waved to me," Mark said proudly. Julia didn't know what to say. She knew that the creatures existed, and that they protected the island. It was a rare thing for one of them to reveal itself to an outsider.

"Mark, I don't think you should tell anyone about this until you have had a chance to talk to Sam," Julia told him.

Chapter Eighteen

"Chief Sinclair, what are you doing over here?" Marie Duval asked as she spied Monica leaving the City Attorney's office.

"Just doing my job, Madame Mayor," Monica replied with a smile, walking on past and out the door. Marie Duval watched her go, frowning. Marie turned and headed for the office that had recently been Lacy Ryan's but now belong to Josie McCoy, one of her hand-picked people. Marie entered without knocking.

"Mayor, I am glad to see you," Josie sighed, standing behind her desk.

"What the devil was Chief Sinclair doing over here?" Marie Duval demanded.

"I was just about to call you. Apparently, she just hired Lacy Ryan's assistant to be her new dispatcher," McCoy snapped angrily, still smarting from the way that Chief Sinclair had talked to her.

Josie McCoy had brown curly hair and big brown eyes, a heart-shaped face and a body built for sin. She was a smart and savvy lawyer, but the Chief of police had rattled her.

"She did what?" Marie Duval was dumbfounded. This was the last move she had expected from the Chief. Kimberly Allen, having worked for Lacy knew more about everything that Lacy had been working on before her death than even she realized.

"I'm pretty sure you heard me the first time. I wanted to pick that girl's brains before I fired her. Now, it looks like I won't get the chance," McCoy growled.

"Don't worry about it. I've made arrangements, we'll be rid of Chief Sinclair soon enough. Once that happens, the sky is the limit, Josie," Marie told her.

"I hope you're right," McCoy told her.

"I'm right. I've been working for this for a long time. I won't let Monica Sinclair stop me," Marie Duval said with conviction.

The Everglades.

Mateo Salvador and his men, those that had survived the storm the previous night, had finally gotten together. The three airboats all were tied together as the criminals tried to come up with a plan to locate and destroy Sam Decker.

"I don't like it out here, Boss. I think it would be better if we took this back into town. We know the streets of Miami a lot better than Decker does," Nico Morales said. He was still unnerved by having to kill several alligators in order for his men to reach their airboat earlier. While he would never admit it to his boss, he hated it out in the swamp. Alligators were the only surviving dinosaurs. He believed that.

They frightened him even more then El Toro. The reptiles of the swamp were killing machines, apex predators of the highest order.

"No!" El Toro shouted. "We must face Decker out here, in the battleground of his choosing. If we do not, then we will be seen as cowards."

"Yes, El Jefe," Morales replied submissively, knowing that now for sure, he would die in this cursed swamp.

"So where do we go, El Jefe?" asked another man.

"We stay here and we let Decker come to us," El Toro said with an air finality.

"Is that what you think is best?"

"It is," Mateo said proudly.

The Everglades covered hundreds of acres of ground. To think that they could sit in one place and be spotted by their enemies, it was preposterous. Except, the men that were chasing them were prepared for the preposterous, and the unexpected.

One of the men had obviously fallen asleep. That was why they had found him on the ground, his throat sliced open and a puddle of blood on the ground below his neck. He had forgotten the first rule of surveillance. Never close your eyes. Now he was dead.

Seminole Joe moved through the 'Glades like a stalking ghost, locating El Toro's men and eliminating all of the perimeter guards. His actions would make it easier for Sam and the others when the time came to attack.

Decker sat silently in the mango tree, his M-16 at the ready. He and Joe had gotten within shooting distance of El Toro, but while Joe was evening up the odds one man at a time, Decker was waiting for everybody else to get in position. Jake and Wally were closed by, and Rafael and John weren't too far out.

The sun was beating down on the swamp, heating up the air. The sun reflecting off the water was taking a toll on the men in the airboats. They were getting sore and irritated and were starting to question the orders of the man that had brought them out into the swamp. That was good for Decker and his friends.

The thing about being out on the water in an alligator-infested swamp is you start to take nature for granted. As long as the alligators aren't attacking you, you tend to forget that they are there. Which is what happened to one of the men in El

Toro's crew who decided to lean out over the edge of the boat and splash some water on his face. At least that was his plan. A passing alligator had other ideas. It shot to the surface, jaws extended and clamped them shut over the man's head and shoulders. With a quick yank, the 'gator pulled the man off the boat and into the water. Two men started shooting into the water, but the body nor the 'gator surfaced. Decker smiled as he listened to the increased grumbling from the two airboats. He also made it a point to check and make sure no slithery critters had decided to visit his tree.

Satisfied that they hadn't, he returned his gaze to the boats. One of El Toro's men, a guy named Nico, started telling the men to be more alert. Yes, they were hot. Yes, they were tired. But they had come out here to do a job! Decker smiled, Nico was going to be really unhappy in about ten minutes.

Enrico Suarez lit a cigarette as he waited in the shade of a mangrove tree. He was beginning to think that coming out into this godforsaken swamp was a wild goose chase. They needed to be back in Miami and getting more product out on the street. People were going crazy over the Flakka. It didn't matter that it turned a lot of them into crazed zombie-like creatures that only wanted to destroy or kill. They *wanted* the rush it gave them, the feeling of having superhuman strength. It was like angel dust times a hundred!

Rico had just taken the cigarette out of his mouth when a hand clamped over his mouth and a cold pain ripped across his throat. In seconds, he was no longer feeling anything. Joe wiped the blood off of his knife on the dead man's shirt and then wedged his arm into the tree to keep him upright to look like he was still alive and on guard. The ear-piece he had informed him that everybody was in position. Joe smiled. It was not a nice thing to see. All hell was about to break loose!

The Island of the Hidden Ones.

Jessica Harmon had just finished another session with Mark Mundy. This was the first time since she had met him that he seemed positive. She wondered why. She went in search of Julia Sinclair.

Julia had just finished a lesson and sent the children out to play in the sunshine. She was watching them through a window when Jessica found her. "Good Morning," Julia greeted her.

"Mark was different this morning," Jessica said, getting straight to the point.

"How so?" Julia asked, curious.

"He seemed almost happy, positive rather than tentative like he has been."

"Well, he got some good news this morning," Julia smiled.

"Which was?" Jessica asked.

"Sam called and spoke to him this morning. He told him that things were almost over and that he would be coming to take him home very soon."

"I'm not sure that is the best thing for him," Jessica sighed.

"Why not?" Julia asked.

"You know what Decker does for a living, right?" Dr. Harmon looked at her.

"Yes, I do. Sam Decker saved my life," Julia said.[3]

"And you think that he is capable of looking out for this child by himself?"

"You might be amazed at the friends that Sam Decker has that are willing to help him with Mark when he is on a case."

"Mark has some serious problems, Julia," Jessica said.

"You don't think I know that? You forget, I'm the one that got you out here."

"Exactly. Sam Decker put his vendetta over taking care of this boy! I can't say that makes him a good candidate as a guardian for Mark."

"What makes you judge and jury, Jessica? What give you the right to decide Mark's future over his father's wishes?"

"Julia, I came because you asked me to. Lacy had set this up before her death. So, I honored my obligation. Now, you want me to step away all because Decker made the boy a promise?"

---

[3] Decker P.I. Smuggler's Blues

"No, Jessica, I want you to give Sam a chance to make good on his promise. He told Mark that he would bring his father's killer to justice. I believe him. Mark does too."

"If the State asks me, at the moment, I am inclined to say that Mark would be better off in foster care," Jessica said.

"That is your opinion. But are you sure that is a fact?" Julia asked.

"I can't say it is a fact. You know that," Jessica sighed.

"Then why don't you back off and give it a chance?"

"I'll think about it."

"That is all I am asking for. For Mark's sake."

Scorpion Cay, Florida Keys.

Myra Dish frowned as she looked at her phone. Apparently, there was a problem with her inquiry into Marie Duval's past. Her immediate supervisor had just texted her to drop it. There was no way in Hell that she was going to do that. Orders or no orders.

Marie Duval was dirty. Myra knew it and she was going to take the Mayor of Scorpion Cay down, one way or another. She dialed Monica Sinclair.

"What have you got, Myra?" Monica asked.

"I was just ordered to drop the investigation into Marie Duval," Myra said.

"Why do you think that happened?" Monica asked.

"I think a larger agency has eyes on her. I'm just not willing to let this go," Myra told her.

"I'd hope not."

"I am not going to let you die," Myra said.

"I appreciate that," Monica told her.

"Let's do this," Decker said into his com unit. He aimed his rifle and pulled the trigger. One of the men on the boat flipped into the water as the bullet removed his head.

He immediately found another target and dispatched it as well. More gunfire erupted and El Toro's men fell. Mateo Salvador spun around as his men dropped around him. Fear filled his belly for the first time since this hunt had started.

Decker and his people were good, better than he had expected. El Toro hit the deck, not caring that his men died around him. He just wanted to live, no matter what!

Decker watched as his men hit the kill squads that had been sent out after them. He made sure that El Toro was the only one that survived. He wanted to make sure that the man that had ordered Lacy's death was going to face the maximum sentence for Murder in the first degree!

Scorpion Cay, Florida Keys.

Myra Dish answered her phone as her fellow agents arrived on the Island. They were happy to back her up, given that the target was a cop. They would not let anything happen to a fellow officer of the law. Once she was sure that they were indeed on the island, Myra dialed Monica's number.

"Yeah, what have you got?" Monica asked.

"I've got people keeping an eye on both your house and your office. Monica, you at the very least are safe," Myra told her.

CHAPTER NINETEEN

Marie Duval made her way to her own office. She found herself wondering what sort of game that the Chief of Police was playing. It was unusual to poach personnel from another city oiffice. Or did Kimberly Allen know something? What had Lacy Ryan told her before her untimely death? That was something that would bear some looking into. The question was how? With Kimberly newly installed on the police department payroll, she couldn't very well summon her to her office to ask questions. Could that be why Chief Sinclair had hired her? It was something to think about.

Myra Dish looked up from her phone as Jeff Conley pulled up beside her. Donnie Cain was with him. She had worked with both agents before and trusted them with her life. She would be trusting them with Monica's life as well. "What's going on,

Myra?" Cain asked from the passenger seat of Conley's car.

"The Mayor has hired the Russians to take out the police chief. Even more oddly, I was told to stand down and stop investigation the acting Mayor of Scorpion Cay," Myra replied. Cain gave a low whistle.

"Yeah that is pretty goddam odd. You think she has an in at Tallahassee?" Conley asked.

"Hard to say. You guys hearing anything about a low-life drug kingpin called El Toro?" Myra asked.

"Shee-it! You bet we have! Ol' El Toro lost two warehouses full of product and his dealers had their supplies of Flakka derstroyed. Word is, he took a small army into the 'glades to chase down the guys that were doing it," Cain chuckled.

"You guys hear about that attorney that got shot at the DEA agent's funeral a couple of weeks back?" Myra asked.

"Yeah, everybody in the state did."

"El Toro was behind it. The lawyer that was killed, she was Sam Decker's fiance."

"That explains a lot," Conley nodded.

"So, how about you enlighten me?" Cain looked over at Conley.

"You ever hear stories about an ex-DEA agent named Sam Decker?" Conley asked.

"Yeah, so?"

"When he left the DEA he became a private eye here on Scorpion Cay."

"Well shit," Cain said.

"Yep. Odds are that El Toro is one dead motherfucker and he don't even know it," Conley told him.

"One other thing, the DEA agent that was killed? He had made Decker the kid's guardian," Myra added.

"I'm glad I'm not El Toro," Cain shook his head.

"Yeah, me too," Conley added. "So Myra, what exactly do you want us to do?"

"I want you two to protect the Police Chief."

"We can do that," Conley nodded.

"You should also know that she dated Decker in the past. So don't fuck up and let anything happen to her. Otherwise, you'll be dealing with Decker," Myra grinned.

"And the news just gets better and better," Conley groaned. Seconds later, the other two FDLE agents backed out of the parking space and headed towards the police station.

The Everglades.

After his last man had fallen, El Toro peered fearfully over the gunwhale of the airboat. He could hear more boats approaching. He had no doubt that Sam Decker would be on one of them. Maybe he would get his chance to kill the gringo pest after all!

If he was going to face death, he would do so on his feet as a man. Even though fear was turning his guts to water, his own code of *machisimo* would not allow him to cower in fear at what he was sure was his impending death. He would meet Sam Decker as a man, not as a coward.

"Mateo, it's been a few days," Sam Decker said as he climbed off his boat and onto the shore of an island. Joe had brought the drug lord on to what was little more than a sawgrass-covered sandspit.

"So now you murder me, Decker? Is that the justice that you so desperately seek?" Mateo Salvador asked.

"Why would I do that when I can put you behind bars for life?" Decker looked amused.

"I don't understand," El Toro looked confused.

"I am here to offer you a chance, Mateo. A chance at life."

"What do you mean?"

"We fight, man to man. The winner walks away, no questions asked," Decker told him.

"And if I win, your friends they will shoot me?"

"Nope. If you win, you walk away. If you lose, you go to jail for as long as I can put you there," Decker replied. El Toro considered his words before speaking.

"I accept your challenge," he said. El Toro figured he had a good chance. He was at least ten years younger than Decker, and he was sure that he was faster and stronger than the private investigator.

"Good enough," Decker told him as he handed off his weapons to the big Indian, and stripped off his tactical vest. Decker stood waiting as El Toro removed his own weapons and shirt. The two men walked towards each other, ready to meet at the center of the sandspit that made up the tiny island they were standing on.

The Island of the Hidden Ones.

Mark Mundy was sitting under a tree by himself when Samantha sat down next to him. "What are you thinking about?" Samantha asked. She was a pretty girl about his own age with long dark hair that hung to her waist. He dark eyes searched his face as she asked her question.

"I was thinking about my Dad, and about Miss Lacy. She was going to be my new Mom before the bad men killed her," Mark replied.

"I lost my parents too," Samantha told him.

"What happened?" Mark was curious.

"My dad got caught by an alligator out in the swamp. My mom caught a fever and died," Samantha said, looking down at her hands in her lap.

"Did that make you sad?" Mark asked.

"It did. It made me sad, and then it made me angry. Why did she have to die? Why couldn't she stay with me?" Samantha asked.

"I don't know," Mark told her honestly.

"I know that too. But we are alike that way. We both lost our parents."

"Yes, we did. Thank you for letting me know I'm not alone."

"I'll always be your friend, Mark."

"And I will always be yours, Samantha."

Miami, Florida.

Dimitri Renko sipped at his water as he sat next to his pool. He had decided not to go into the officer today and instead take this very important meeting at his home. Borya Yakov walked out of the house and into the sunlight. He wore white pants and shoes, a pale green shirt with the tails hanging out. An expensive wrist watch adorned his left wrist and dark aviator style sunglasses covered his eyes. His dark hair was razor-cut and expensively styled. He walked over and sat down in a chair next to Renko, pleased to be under the shade of the umbrella. A servant approached and put a glass bottle of Perrier water on the table next to him before disappearing back inside.

"You have work for me?" Yakov asked.

"Yes." Renko replied, pulled a cigar from his pocket and biting off the end. He spat it into a small trash container next to his chair before putting the cigar in his lighter and firing it up. He pulled a second one out and offered it to Yakov, but he declined.

"What is the job?" Yakov asked.

"There is a cop that is being a problem for one of my associates down in the Keys. She needs to be eliminated," Renko said.

"The target, the cop, is a woman?"

"Yes. Chief Monica Sinclair of the Scorpion Cay police department."

"I don't much like killing women."

"That is why I am willing to pay five million dollars American for the job. Will that amount sooth your conscience?"

"It should do nicely. For a woman, I require full amount up front."

"Why not the usual terms?"

"Because target is a woman," Yakov said.

"Very well. Check your accounts in an hour," Renko said.

"A pleasure doing business," Yakov replied, standing and walking out, leaving his bottle of water untouched. Renko watched him go, frowning as he did so. He hadn't realized that Borya was such a sentimentalist. He would bear watching on this job.

Borya Yakov exited Dimitri Renko's home. He did not like targeting women. It went back to the way that his mother had suffered at the hands of an abusive husband and father. That was why he had demanded the full payment up front. Five million dollars was a lot of money. Renko hadn't batted and eye, which meant that he could have asked for more.

That bothered him more than anything else. It meant that Renko was desperate. Why was that?

The Everglades.

Sam Decker ducked beneath El Toro's swing and sent a hard right into the drug dealer's gut, doubling him over. He followed with a left cross across the chin that sent Mateo Salvador staggering backward. The drug lord spat blood and charged forward again. He swung a roundhouse right that Decker ducked under and the former DEA agent slammed a hard-knuckled fist into the drug lord's ribs. The snap of bone was loud, and as the two men stepped backwards, Salvador spat more blood. His breathing sounded labored.

Decker let Salvador charge before launching a side kick that folded Salvador in the middle. The drug lord puked up blood before launching himself at Decker once more. Sam met the charge with a doubled fist that dropped him to the sand. "It's time to pay the piper, Mateo," Decker told him. Mateo Salvador collapsed onto the sand.

Sam Decker stood over him, breathing heavily. The fight had taken a toll on him. El Toro was beaten. Lacy had been avenged. Sam stood by as Rafael cuffed Mateo Salvador and headed him towards one of the boats. Now they would take him back to Miami to stand trial. Decker wouldn't actually be a part of that, but that was okay. He had a couple of promises to keep first!

Island of the Hidden Ones.

Mark had left Samantha. He liked her, but he also was nervous around her. She knew what he was going through, but he found himself liking her maybe just a little too much. He would talk to Dr. Harmon about her and see what she thought.

The Everglades.

"You did good, Sammy," Wally Norwood told him.

"Why is that, Wally?" Decker asked.

"Because you didn't kill him, Sammy."

"I guess that is something, isn't it?" Decker looked at the man that had been his substitute father.

"It is a whole lot more than you think."

"I hope so, Wally. I really do," Decker told him.

"So, are we done out here?" Rafael asked, looked at his friend.

"With this part of it anyway. How about you and John deliver this guy to the cops back in Miami. I've got a promise to keep," Decker said.

"Okay, we can do that," Rafael Cortez nodded. John Longfellow looked relieved. Wally slapped Decker on the back and helped Rafael gather the prisoner and guide him towards one of the airboats.

"Joe, let's go pick up Mark," Decker said.

"Yes, it is time," Joe nodded.

CHAPTER TWENTY

Scorpion Cay, Florida Keys.

      Borya Yakov drove his rental car off the ferry and into the Scorpion Cay Marina parking area. He located a parking space and pulled into it. He then used his iPhone to pull up Google Earth so he could take a look at the island and make plans for the touch.

Borya was former Soviet *Spetsnaz*, a feared member of the Russian GRU's Special Forces. After the fall of the Soviet Union he was released from service. His skills were marketable to the right people. He discreetly put out the word that his skills were for sale if the price was right.

A Saudi Prince was having trouble with a desert shiek. Borya took care of it. After that, his skills were much in demand. His Swiss bank accounts grew. Finally, he was offered permanent employment with Dimitri Renko with additioinal benefits. Now Renko had given him this job.

To Borya, it was distasteful. He didn't like making war on women or children. This police person, was a woman. Still, it w2as the job that he was being paid to do. First, he needed to get a good look at her and follow her to get a sense of her routine. He looked up the location for the combination Police Station/jail. He backed his car out and headed into the city proper of Scorpion Cay.

Conley and Cain had reached the police station and set up on opposite sides of the block where they could maintain a vigil on both the front and the back. Myra had provided them both with a picture of Monica Sinclair so they would know her when they saw her. They had grabbed sandwiches from McDonalds before heasding to the Police Station.

"You think the guy may try to hit her here?" Cain asked.

"At this point, nothing would surprise me. Right now, we watcvh for anything that seems out of place," Conley replied, lighting a cigarette as he spoke.

The Everglades, the island of the Hidden Ones.

"How are you doing today, Mark?" Jessica Harmon asked. It was getting into the afternoon, not long after lunch. It was a time when most everyone on the island was resting, making it a perfect time for her to talk to Mark alone.

"I'm okay, I guess," Mark shrugged.

"You guess? What do you mean by that?" Jessica asked him.

"I—I made a friend today. Her name is Samantha. She lost her parents too."

"So that is something that you both have in common. Did she talk to you about how she felt about losing her parents?"

"Yes."

"How did that make you feel, Mark?"

"It made me feel…odd." Mark replied.

"What do you mean, odd?" Jessica asked.

"I like Samantha. She is maybe the first real friend that I have made since I came here. I want to help her not feel bad."

"That is a good thing, Mark. I'm glad you want to help her."

There was a knock on the door. Mark and Jessica both turned to look at the door as it swung open. Sam Decker stepped inside. "Mister Sam!

Mark shouted happily as he charge him. Sam Decker scooped him up in a hug and held the boy tight.

"It's over now, Mark. The man responsible for killing your dad and Miss Lacy is on his way to jail as we speak," Decker told the boy.

"Thank you, Mr. Sam!"

"Just call me Sam, Mark."

"Can we go home now?" Mark asked.

"We can. Who is your friend?" Decker asked, nodding towards Jessica Harmon.

"That is Doctor Harmon. Miss Julia called her here to help me," Mark explained.

"Doctor Harmon, I'm Sam Decker," he introduced himself.

"I've heard a lot about you, both from Mark and Julia and Rick Marlow," Jessica said.

"I'm sure you have. I want to thank you for the help you have given Mark."

"He needs to keep seeing me," Jessica said.

"I'm sure that he does. I can drive him down to Key West to see you, or you are more than welcome to come to our house on Scorpion Cay," Decker told her.

"Oh, I certainly want to see where Mark is going to be living at," Jessica said. She could tell that Decker could be very disarming where women were concerned.

"I'm glad to hear it. I know that Lacy, my fiance, had called you before her untimely death.

Thank you for taking the time to follow up with Mark," Decker told her.

"Mark is a good kid, the pleasure was all mine," Jessica told him.

"Glad to hear it. I need to take him back home now. Is that okay? Do you need a ride back out of the swamp?" Decker asked her.

"I could certainly use one. Have you told Julia Sinclair that you are here to take Mark back home?"

"Not yet, but I will be more than happy to," Decker said with a smile.

"For some reason, that doesn't surprise me."

"I never worked in the shadows. I work with what I know," Decker shrugged.

"In other words, Damn the torpedoes and full speed ahead!"

"Pretty nice, Decker," Julia said. She had come up behind him and watched the interaction between Decker, Mark, and Doctor Harmon.

"I was just about to come looking for you, and let you know that it is over and it's safe for Mark to come home," Decker smiled at her.

"Joe beat you too it."

"Leave it to Joe to spoil a surprise."

"Can I talk to you for a few minutes in private?" Julia asked.

"Sure thing. Mark, you continue your talk with Doctor Harmon, okay?"

"Yes, Mr. Sam," Mark replied. Decker followed Julia outside into the sunlight.

"What's up, Julia?" Decker asked as the heat dropped on them like a wet blanket.

"You are going to have to win Dr. Harmon over, Sam. She's all but made up her mind that you aren't fit to be Mark's guardian. She told me that last night," Julia explained.

"She'll have hell to pay stopping me," Decker said coldly.

"I know that too, Sam. But right now, you've got to turn on the charm and win her over before you leave here with Mark," Julia hugged him. Decker hugged her back.

"I'll do my best."

Miami, Florida. DEA Headquarters.

Dan Costa was waiting at the front door when Wally Norwood, Joihn Longfellow, Rafael Cortez, and a handcuffed Mateo Salvador arrived. "How's Decker?"

"Alive and well. He sent you this present," Wally grinned.

"Mateo Salvador, you are under arrest for the murder of Kyle Mundy and Lacy Ryan," Costa informed him. Two uniformed police officers took posession of him and hustled him inside. Tell Decker I owe him one."

"I certainly will," Rafael nodded. "Gentlemen, it is time to go home."

"Yes it is," John Longfellow added. They headed back to their respective vehicles.

Scorpion Cay, Florida Keys.

Myra Dish continued to keep an eye on the Mayor. If she proved to be wrong on this, her ass was going to be in a sling for sure. Conley and Cain along with her. Her gut told her that the Mayor was dirty. Now she had to get the proof of it without sacrificing Chief Sinclair's life. Fuck it, it was time to rattle the Mayor's cage. Myra climbed out of her car and headed for the Mayor's office.

Being out of the car was a little cooler but not by much. The sun was blazing hot as it beat down on the pavement and reflected back up at her. An iguana crawled from bushes lining the walk to crawl up on a rock to sun itself. She pushed open the door to the city building. Cold air washed over her, quickly drying the sweat on her skin.

Her heels clacked on the floor as she made her way to the elevator. A directory next to it gave the location of the Mayor's office. Myra hit the button for the Mayor's floor. The doors closed behind her and the elevator began to rise. Seconds later, Dish stepped out on the Mayor's floor. She wasn't aware of the four white SUV's that had pulled up in the parking lot outside. A woman in a white pantsuit with short dark hair stepped out. She was obviously in charge based on the way that the men in SWAT uniforms deferred to her. Together they started for the front of the building.

Myra pushed open the door to the outer office. An older blonde woman sat at a desk there. "May I help you?" she asked.

"Special Agent Myra Dish, FDLE to see the Mayor please," Myra informed her.

"I'll let her know that you are here," the woman said. The nameplate on her desk identified her as Roberta Simms.

Myra nodded and waited. A few seconds later, Roberta opened the door and Myra stepped in to be face to face with Marie Duval. Mayor Duval looked up from the papers that were spread across her desk. "What can I do for you, Agent Dish?" she asked.

"How was dinner with Dimitri Renkov?" Myra asked. Marie Duval paled, her face losing color.

"I have no idea what you are talking about," Marie said, but her eyes told a different story.

"Yes you do," Dish dismissed her statement.

"You hired an assassin to kill the Mayor. I observed the whole thing," Dish told her.

"How?"

"I was in the restaurant with you."

"Well, you are wrong," Marie said dismissively.

"No, I'm not. The FBI is already in the building. They have it all on audio," Myra told her.

"You are full of shit!" Marie rolled her eyes.

"I'm afraid not," Kendall Royce said as she pushed her way into the office. Thanks to S.A. Dish, we were able to get a warrant to bug the restaurant last night ahead of time. We have the whole meeting on record," Special Agent Kendall Royce announced.

"You can't stop what I've put in motion," Marie shook her head.

"Yes, we can. And we have. Borya Yakov is being arrested as we speak," Royce said sweetly.

"This isn't over," Marie Duval snarled.

"Yes, Marie, it is," Dish told her.

A week later...

This is a good time, Sam," Wally Norwood told him.

"Yes it is," Decker agreed. He was watching Mark play with Nora's kids in the backyard of his recently rebuilt home. Mark had filled out a lot, once he was eating regular again., Joe had brought Samantha from the Isle of the Hidden Ones, and she and Mark were almost inseperable. Julia Sinclair had come along as well.

"You have done a good thing for Mark, Sam," Julia told him.

"That means a lot coming from you, Julia," Decker told her.

"Did you know that the FBI was going after the Mayor?" Julia asked.

"I had no clue. It seems Monica did, however. Her and Agent Dish have become really close," Decker noted.

"Yes they have. How about you, Sam? Is there anyone you are interested in?" Julia asked, looking into his eyes.

"Maybe. But if there is, I need to take it slow. Not just for my sake, but for Mark's as well," Decker said.

"You'll manage," Julia smiled at him.

"I'm sure I will," Decker told her, smiling back.

Sam Decker will return.

Author's Note:

I know that this book was a long time coming out after Those Left Behind. I had to make sure that I was getting the character of Mark Mundy just right in the way that he would be dealing with the murder of two people that he cared a lot about, happening right in front of him. Kids are resilient, they bounce back much faster than adults. However, some things are harder to process than others. I want to thank therapist Dick Rogers and Courtney Cromas of the Kane, Loveridge Medical Group for their help in getting into Mark's head and into Decker's as well. To those who waited, thanks for reading!